THE MEN ABOUT MY TOWN

Thomas O'Lorr

The men about my town by Thomas O'Lorr

Published by: Thomas O'Lorr

Cover and design by Thomas O'Lorr

Copyright © 2021 Thomas O'Lorr

ISBN: 978-1-7399421-0-6

www.thomasolorr.co.uk

1st EDITION

Her words surfaced from my mind's abyss:
A man like you will die alone.

Content Notes:

This book contains foul language, sex/nudity, violence.

Dear Reader,

My real name is not Thomas O'Lorr. I chose to write this book under a pseudonym to protect the identity of my loved ones. I now live in London, but I was born and raised Romanian. As you might know, homophobia occupies a high position in any statistics in my country, and I found it crucial to keep my identity hidden. I hope you'll understand.

Even though the story is a work of fiction and my imagination had a high input in creating this book, I managed to sew in my reality and past experiences so that you might learn a thing or two from my mistakes. I'm not here to advise you on how to live your life. I'm just telling the story of Thomas, the man how wanted freedom.

You might wonder why I have chosen the name *Thomas O'Lorr,* but couldn't think of a better one to rhyme with "Oh, Lord!"

I hope you enjoy reading this story as much as I did writing it, and if you do, feel free to share it with the world!

Best wishes,

Thomas O'Lorr

PS: If you are a man, make sure to hide your erection if you read this book in public.

One

The first sight of the British sky was breathtaking, and I couldn't believe how low the clouds seemed; you could almost stretch your arm towards them and play your fingers through the marshmallow beauty of an autumn welkin. My first memory of the United Kingdom, the place I would call home from then on. I was sat on the rare sits of the coach next to the toilet, clutching my backpack while trying to compose myself and come back to reality.

The past couple of months had had their toll on me with an avalanche of emotions that exhausted me physically and mentally. My spirit was shattered by a lifetime of internal struggles that reached their peak. In vain farewells and forget-me-not flowers were already sinking in mud and dragging me with them. The feeling of trashed emotions slowly converted my excitement into fear. Finally, I shook my head in a last desperate attempt to power through my feelings and enjoy the prospect of a promising new life.

I turned my head to check on Carmen, the crazy one who packed her bags and moved to London with me. I couldn't apprehend at that time what made her run almost 2000 miles across the world with me, a stranger. I simply thought she was as fed up and tired of Romania as I was. Her face was chalk-white, with dark circles contouring her empty eyes. She scrutinized the horizon through the dusty windows taking no notice of me. I later found out how much of a crush Carmen had on me. The same thing that made her leave her family and friends behind would push us on separate paths a year later. The vertigo state I found myself in lasted as long. I was a cocktail of dreams and hopes mixed with a dash

7

of hatred, few leaves of jealousy for garnish, and spiked with a thousand and one gay skeletons in the closet. It sounds like the perfect concoction for an ideal start of a new life. But, in all fairness, it was this or me hanging at the end of a rope.

I fell asleep during the ride, and when I woke up, we entered Victoria Coach Station. From here, the remaining four steps out of my unwritten five-step plan, the first one was making it into London, were straightforward: buy an Oyster card, find the hotel we booked for three nights, rent a room for the two of us and get a job. If I knew that all of this would happen in this order, maybe I would have focused and prioritized it differently. But, unfortunately, I was never good at making plans that worked, and contouring this was my way of facing the uncertainty which shrouded what turned out to be a one-way life-changing trip.

The hotel was located in Crystal Palace, and making my way there wasn't an easy job. I stuffed thirty kilograms of essential belongings in a cheap suitcase that lost its wheels the moment I got off the bus, and I found myself dragging it on the sidewalks ripping off its fabric, almost losing my outdated underwear.

After checking in, all we wanted was a beer, a smoke, and some food. And to sleep. While sat on the hotel's terrace with a drink and a cigarette in my hand, I looked at Carmen, questioning my decisions, and realized how reckless I was two months before embarking on this journey. I had nothing in common with the person in front of me. I barely knew her, and all I learned came from the stories we shared over drinks in the six months we worked together. At that moment, the comprehending of the state I was in made itself evident. I left my comfort zone to pursue the freedom lacking in my country, to be one with the person I kept hidden inside of me for a lifetime, putting all my trust in a stranger, being deluded that my safety net was weaved between her and my parents.

I wasn't in a safe place financially, and this aspect of my life shadowed my mental health and implicitly my thoughts and actions. I made two wedding cakes for some of my brother's friends and overcharged for them to afford to move to London. Additionally, I managed to save a more significant percentage of my last two salaries. When the community spirit in my hometown materialized in cash, a couple of neighbors gave me £200 as a farewell gift. This brought me to a total of £1000. It was more than I ever had in my pocket at any given point in my five years as part of the working class. I thought that this would be more than enough to make it here and, oh boy, couldn't be more wrong. Just in the first three days, I've spent £300 on a hotel, travel card, and necessities like beer and food. You might wonder why I'm rambling about my financial status, and here's the reason: if you are someone who dreams of moving somewhere, make sure you do it after you've secured a job and accommodation because it is not fun *hun*.

Always judging myself and my ability to do things properly, I refused to speak English when I had someone around to do it for me. And that someone was Carmen. As a result, she was in charge of emailing and calling landlords and arranging house viewings with them. We were in such a rush to find a cheap room and stop paying for the hotel that in three days, we managed to move my broken suitcase, outdated underwear, and her quality girly stuff in a shared three-bedroom flat on Forest Road in the sunny and dusty Walthamstow.

We got to share a small double room in a house owned by an Indian couple. They occupied what was supposed to be the living room. The other room was rented by an unnamed

Lithuanian girl whose soul pleasures were midnight cooking and loud sex with multiple partners. Oh, how much I envied her. At times I imagined myself being a voyeur, sitting on an armchair in the corner of her room, cock in hand, watching the men fucking the brains out of her. The screams and moans I had to put up with awaken the burning desire for sexual freedom and orgasmic satisfaction, all of which I forgot about during the first two weeks in the UK.

The first one to find a job was Carmen. After updating her living status on Facebook, an old acquaintance of hers got in contact. We went out for a boring catch-up and few drinks with him at the local pub up the road from our place. Two days later, he arranged an interview for her at his workplace. Not long after, she got hired as a waitress in a private member's club in Piccadilly Circus. It was my luck as much as hers. She made money now to pay the rent, which was a relief. I would pay her back the moment I found a job.

I almost gave up and was willing to adopt the title of Sir Failure and move back to Romania, apologize to my boss at the restaurant in Brasov and beg him to take me back. I failed two trial shifts for chef de parties positions in posh restaurants, mainly due to my understanding of the language and its regional accents and dialects. I got so scared that my dream of building a life in a more open-minded and varied environment than communist-stained Romania was turning into a nightmare. To this day, I make a weekly note to myself to stop being such a dreamer. Life isn't just a piece of cake, and if it is, well, it is served with a cup of salted coffee. So with this cloud raining on my parade, I went for a walk to clear my head and stop crying before going home to meet the most accomplished of them all – Carmen.

The October weather was surprisingly good, comparing it with my expectations regarding the cold, wet climate on the island. Unguided and entirely out of touch with my surroundings, I turned left through an opening in a metal fence and found myself for the first time in Lloyd Park. How come I wasn't aware of the existence of it? It was literary a couple of hundred meters from my flat. Smoking cigarette after cigarette, contemplating my failures, and pushing myself further down than I already was, I noticed a coffee shop located at the back of William Morris Gallery and decided to spend my last four pounds on a coffee. I had given up at that point. I was a failure. I tried composing a pledge to my parents to buy me a one-way ticket back home but had no idea how to deliver it.

I reluctantly entered the coffee shop playing with the change in my pocket when, I noticed on the counter a spread of sweets: carrot cake with cream cheese frosting, brownies, blondies, crafted granola bars, scones, and a selection of yogurt and granola pots with fruits and other purees, and found myself asking the girl at the till if they have any openings in their production kitchen. In a way, baffled by my question, she handed me an obsolete business card and told me to call a number written on it in pencil.

A phone call and an email later, I was scheduled for an interview at 4 pm the next day. Five days later, I had a trial shift that resulted in me getting a pastry chef job for a corporate catering company. Thus, the sun has risen on my street and shined brighter than ever. My dreams were still valid.

To confirm and make an official statement of my success in London, I updated my Facebook status. When I thought I knew no one besides Carmen so far from home, an old acquaintance sends me a message and asks to meet him for a beer the next day, which I welcomed wholeheartedly. Coincidence or not, we had the same name, Thom.

The last time I've heard of him was when my best friend Maria told me in a gossip frenzy that he moved to Malta to be with his brother, who was going through a divorce. I knew him from college. He was a year older than me. Thanks to being part of the same social group, I got to know him quite well during those years. That group consisted of twenty-five mixed individuals calling themselves *friends*, and somehow I never felt fully included but tolerated. Most of them were bullies of mine back in primary school, an aggregation of undefeatable archenemies. A bunch of cunts who were no longer part of my life. And I was grateful for it.

Carmen and I met him near Harrods. He was waiting for his girlfriend, Suzanna, to finish work and join us. Somehow, the reunion was neutral from my side, while he seemed thrilled to have met me. Thom was a fine-looking guy, tall, athletic, with short curly brown hair and eyes of the same color. Back in college, he dated for six years Antoinette, one of my good friends. Thom dedicated all this time solely to her. Still, when success in sports and later in the business world found him, he broke up with her leaving behind a damaged girl aged 25 who struggled to recover from a heartbreak so awful that put her in a mental hospital for four months.

"In my defense, I must tell you that I never intended to hurt her. I was going through a challenging time in my life. My football career ended due to a knee injury which consequently led to me losing my scholarship. My bar struggled more and more to make ends meet while I have fallen prey to beautiful, hot women wanting to sleep with me", Thom told me a few months later when I confronted him with what I've learned about Antoinette's misfortunes.

The three of us were having a smoke on the side of the road and catching up with each one's journey to London when Suzanna showed up. She was 29 years old, of Polish nationality, blonde with blue eyes and ivory skin, dressed tidy, wearing a subtle but noticeable perfume. She interrupted our conversation by saying a cheerful *hello* while jumping into Thom's arms, kissing him lovingly. The introductions were made in English, which was suspicious at that time, knowing that Thom's girlfriend Suzanna was a girl he met in his glorious years in Bucharest. It turned out that the latter charmed him back in Malta while they spent their free time together, sunbathing on the beach, drinking, or smoking weed. She appeared funny and curious, enquiring how Carmen and I met, how we moved to England together, where we lived and worked. The usual questions one asks when meeting another for the first time.

As the sun was setting, it started raining. The buzzing city became louder and busier instantly, like an ant colony making its way back to the anthill at the beginning of summer rain. One never notices how red and shiny Piccadilly Circus becomes on a rainy day. The lights reflecting in the wet streets converted the surroundings into an apocalyptic turmoil of cars and people rushing by, and I with them, ignoring the ever-growing screams for help of the buskers singing at a corner of a street.

We found shelter in a gothic-themed pub's garden on Frith Street.

The working man, Thom, paid that time, considering I hadn't started my job yet. I promised to cover the bill the next time we met, from my first salary.

I was more of a spectator at the fiery conversations. Suzanna wanted me to speak in English, so I toned down my chattiness due to my reluctance, slipping away from the fun and denying my impulse to present an opinion on the debated subjects. Carmen got charmed by them during this time, and not long after we made our way home, she told me how nice it would be to meet them more often.

Two

The first few months unfolded without a notable incident. After the impasse on finding a job, I went into a state of numbness. Still, the image of me back home, lying on my kitchen floor suffering my first ever panic attack, was omnipresent and became an earthed pillar upon which I wanted to build my brand new free life at any cost.

I'm grateful now for having Carmen as my friend and companion in this endeavor, though at that moment, her presence in my life was a burden, and she was part of the collateral damage my life-long secret created.

I am homosexual. I like men and everything they have: strong arms, firm and hairy chests and bodies, hilly buttocks, and protrusive cocks. I love cocks. Dicks. Penises! I knew this about me, and I knew it well, and yet, all composed the forbidden fruit I craved.

In the beginning, I haven't taken notice of Carmen. She didn't irritate me. On the night we shook hands and concreted the plan to move to London, I haven't noticed the spark in her eyes. Or the night she came home after her first pay in London and surprised me with tickets for Imagine Dragons live at the O2, I haven't noticed the joy she exhaled in the dusty darkened room, nor I cared for when she cooked for me for the first (and last) time. I was too selfish and concerned with myself to notice her love. I was a cunt, and I couldn't have done much about it anyway.

For nine months I shared a bed with her, and as the days went by, I became more and more aware of the love she nurtured for me, and it scared me.

Growing up in an environment where I wasn't validated by society marked me. I had to suppress my feelings and desires just to shape the mask of survival. This turned into my coping mechanism in a world full of hate and judgements. So how could I come to terms with my pathetic existence and confess to Carmen who I am and, at the same time, keep myself protected from the shame outing of my greatest secret can bestow upon me? I couldn't find a way to come to terms with my weak self, so I just ignored the hints and glimmers of love she threw my way.

With time, our conversations diminished, our friendship faded away. I felt the need to be next to Carmen, support her as much as possible and repay her for everything she has done for me in the first month in London. I made a promise to her, and to myself, to support each other and be there for one another in times of trouble, and I planned to keep my word, but it wasn't easy.

Being the only child of a highly competitive couple, Carmen got neglected by her parents on their way to success. She had been raised by her maternal grandparents, for whom she had love and respect, but blamed her parents for every single bad thing that happened to her. To overcompensate for their absence in her forming years, they never denied her a thing. Even though they had extramarital relationships and dreamed of having different lives, her parents got stuck in a marriage on which they worked hard to maintain for the sake of their daughter. Carmen knew of this, and she played it to her advantage. They gave her whatever she wanted.

To punish them, growing up, Carmen took the path of the rebel child, a teenager for which life has no meaning and only long nights drinking and smoking weed made sense. Then, when she turned twenty-three and finished her studies, she realized that she was slowly abandoned by her drinking buddies, exchanging pints for nappies, meaningless sex for a nine-to-five job, and wasted time in bars for quiet evenings home with their families. This wake-up call pushed her to make a change, so she clenched at me and my desperate attempt to run away from my life.

It was fun and pleasant at times to have someone close to whom I can turn and say a word or a joke, to fill the space I found myself in – no friends nor family around that I can lean on but forever in love with me, Carmen.

When we first arrived at our residence on Forest Road, the room we rented was cold and dark, but it was all we could afford at that time. This dungeon was located at the end of a long hallway next to the bathroom in a three-bedroom flat. We found so much dark, long hair inside the room that we believed the previous tenant to be cousin It from Addams Family, who died and disintegrated there. It took us around four hours to clean and make the room comfortable to sleep in. It wasn't much, it was all we had, and whatever I tried to do to make it feel like home, it never did.

I missed having privacy. From living by myself for the last two years, in a rented studio flat in Brasov, I ended up sharing a room, even worst, the bed with a woman, a woman that wanted more than to rest on the same sheets with me.

After a couple of months from our arrival, Carmen took a four-day holiday to Romania to visit her parents, which made me feel relief. I was so eager to be by myself. I was so horny. My balls were hurting me while my prostate begged for attention.

I was twenty-five and a virgin. I have never been with a woman nor a man.

In my teenage years, I was introduced to the euphoric self-induced state of pleasure during a sleepover at one of my friend's houses. Marian and I were classmates, and our parents, friends.

That evening, we went to sleep late, taking advantage of the freedom of having the house to ourselves, with no adult to tell us what to do. After changing in pajamas, we sat in bed under the same duvet when suddenly Marian asked me:

"Have you ever masturbated?"

"Yes," I answered, trying to compose myself and stop my voice from shaking with surprise. I didn't want him to think less of me; never having a male best friend, I didn't want to seem less in his eyes and make him disregard me as a companion.

"After midnight, there is a porn program on TV that we can watch and maybe wank together? What do you think?"

"Of course!" I replied, suppressing my excitement.

"Was this what teenage guys do when they have sleepovers?" I asked myself. Either way, I was thrilled. This would be the first time I saw another guy's penis, and I was only thirteen.

And so it happened. Ten minutes past midnight, after rigorous searching through TV channels, we stumbled upon a porn movie, and so I came to see for the first time a man in action. His muscular body veiled in sweat made my penis twitch. He penetrated a blonde woman in the ass with a long thick cock making her scream with pain and pleasure. My heart started beating fast, and I could feel my cock swelling and ejecting pre-cum, making me uncomfortable. I felt ashamed. I couldn't find the courage to turn and face Marian, nor to utter a word. Thankfully, he spoke first:

"Look at that ass! He's ruining her with that cock. I hope mine will grow as big as that. I want to do to girls what he does to her! How big is yours? Let me see. Are you turned on yet?"

I turned my head to face him and saw Marian, cock in hand, stroking it. Our eyes met, and I noticed a cheeky smile on his face. "Come on," he said, "show me your dick!"

Nervously, I moved aside the duvet and pulled it out. In the dim light cast by the TV, my cock shone with clammy cum. He let go of his penis and stretched his arm towards mine, asking if he can touch it. He didn't wait for an answer and grabbed it gently, pulling my foreskin down revealing the wet knob. Shivers ran through my body while he lightly passed his thumb over the slippery head.

"Your cock is great… thicker than mine," he said while squeezing and moving his hand up and down the shaft, increasing the speed with every stroke. Then, in a soft voice, he asked me to do the same to him, and I did.

We didn't last long. I came first, and Marian followed shortly. We wiped the semen on a T-shirt abandoned on the armchair in the corner of the room, pledged to never speak about this ever again, and went to sleep. But, of course, I couldn't sleep straight away. I felt lightheaded with delight, still feeling the reminisce of his grasp on my cock. I had so many unanswered questions, but the one prevailing was how one could have anal sex without shitting? But all was answered with a quick search on the internet.

Carmen left for the airport early morning on a Thursday, which gave me a full four days of privacy. I still had to work until Friday, but I had the evenings to watch porn and wank in peace.

While having my morning coffee that Saturday, I had an idea: because I couldn't feel comfortable douching in the flat while the landlady and the Lithuanian girl were home, I booked a cheap hotel room somewhere in South Woodford. My plan was simple: go to the nearest sex shop and purchase a dildo, then head to the hotel where I can spend the night watching porn and pleasure myself.

I never owned a dildo. Back home, buying one was too risky and too expensive to make such a purchase. So I ended up using a makeshift one, built of cardboard and paper, glued together in a cylindric shape on which I slipped two condoms. I called it George, and I used it for years. But now was the time to experience a more close to nature one.

Said and done, I packed a change of clothes and some snacks in a backpack and headed to the sex shop. It wasn't far from the house, so I walked there. It gave me the much-needed time to compose myself and not look nervous in front of the shop assistant and think of a speech if small talk was required at the till.

The shop was obscure, on the main street, and not hosting a large selection of toys. Before arriving there, I've set a budget of £30 for the sake of not spending all my money in one weekend. The store was empty, with a mid-age man behind the till who greeted me and offered his assistance. I politely declined with a nod of my head and went browsing the shelves. The shop's content was dedicated to male customers, with a large selection of magazines, DVDs, condoms, and lubes displayed all around the place. In a far corner on the bottom two shelves, I found on display six dildos and four vibrators varying in size and shape. Carefully I picked up the merchandise, trying to see if any of the dildos resembled Gorge, my home-crafted shlong.

Unwilling to spend more than five minutes inside the store, out of fear of being seen there (like anyone around who could recognize me – I was so paranoid!), I grabbed the one priced at £28.99. It was a seven-inch soft, black silicone toy. I paid for it while pretending not to speak or understand a word of English and stormed out of the store, not looking back.

A couple of hours later, around 3 pm, I checked in at the hotel's reception. All went smoothly, but all this adventure had a toll on me. I found myself mentally exhausted, crippled by the fear of being seen or recognized by one of the ten people I knew in London. I went to my room, unboxed the dildo just to realize that the seven inches of promised heaven came in a thin shape — a disappointment. I liked them thick.

I went through with my plan anyway. I jumped in the shower, where meticulously I unscrewed the showerhead, made sure the water was lukewarm and running without significant pressure before gently pressing the end of the hose in my butthole. I could feel the warm water feeling my rectum and passing in my colon, causing my belly to bloat. When I couldn't keep it in any longer, I lowered myself in the bathtub letting the feces-charged liquid burst out of me like a geyser. I repeated this for few times until the water came out clean. Then I showered and decided to take a nap before the big night.

It wasn't a restful sleep. I tossed and turned for an hour, feeling cramps building up inside my belly. I was so tired, and it was so painful that I decided to let go of what I hoped was just an innocent fart. But, to my surprise, the geyser was still active. It built up the reminiscence of douching and exploded on the white cotton bedding creating an impressive piece of art worth displaying in Tate Modern.

I was shocked and didn't know if I should laugh or cry. I jumped off the bed, brown water trickling down my inner thighs, and stripped the sheets off. I went into the bathroom, turned on the water in the bathtub, and tried washing off the mess. All I did was to make it worse. The beautiful white of the bedding turned a pale yellow under the hot water stream, and minutes later, I decided to stop and hang them to dry on the shower's curtain pole.

Even though my appetite for sex disappeared after this unfortunate event, I didn't want to waste the opportunity to pleasure myself. I attempted another short rinse of my rectum, searched for a porn movie, and laid down on a towel on the bathroom floor. I couldn't even conceive of doing this in the stripped bed, right on the mattress. I played the porn. It featured Rocco Steel, a hunk of a man that gets my motor running just upon hearing his deep husky voice, not to mention seeing his majestic phallus. I spat on the dildo and slowly pushed it inside me. It felt like meeting an old friend from whom I straightened ages ago. My sphincter battled the toy's girth, confused by the slow motion of penetration, not knowing if to relax or tighten. I pushed it deeper and deeper, inserting it to the limit, slowly exciting the prostate. I could feel a build-up of precum driving through my flaccid cock.

Opening my eyes, I watched the moaning bottom crushed by Rocco's powerful thrust and tried to synchronize with them. Unexpectedly, I felt a painful cramp followed by a charge of soft brown matter that pushed the toy out of me and splashed my surroundings dirtying the towel and the bathroom floor. I couldn't believe it! I didn't know at that time how important the diet and the break between an enema and anal penetration were for one who bottoms. Learn from one's mistakes! It's all I'm saying. I stopped and sat on the toilet, head in hands, thinking of my misery and stupidity, of how lame and weak I was and how I managed to resume such disgraceful and pitiful actions. How the sexual urges prevailed and pushed me to succumb, exposing myself to shame and undoubtedly criticism and ridicules on behalf of those that one day might find out who I am and what I did.

The room looked as ripped from the pages of a script of a horror film - *The murder of the Poop Monster*. Lured in a hotel room, the deceased, under the promise of joy, got slaughtered with a jet of water that scattered his remains all over the place – a movie I would watch.

I felt so ashamed of the state of the room, so I tried to clean the crime scene as best I could.

I left the room hoping that the bed sheets and towel will dry by the time the housekeeping came in to clean and prepare the lodging for the future guest.

"Will they figure me out? Will they go and check who checked in that room? Will they care? Have they seen worse than this?" - I kept asking myself this, over and over again, while making my way back to the room on Forest Road. I discarded the dildo in a bin on a dark street corner, neatly wrapped in the 5p bag I used to carry my snacks. I had to dispose of the murder weapon… and the motive.

I spent that Sunday curled up in bed, watching movies and feeling sorry for myself, having flashbacks of the room covered in my waste.

Three

That year, Carmen and I spent Christmas at Lena, Suzanna's sister. Thom's brother, Adrian, and his son joined us. It was the saddest winter holiday I ever experienced. My mental health was on the rocks. I felt like an autumn leaf, falling lifeless from a tree that didn't want me. I was swept away by a cold wind, never to touch the ground I most desired, the place where I could rest and decay peacefully in the company of those like me.

Not a stranger to wearing a mask and faking a good mood, I propped up a smile and joined the fun. My English improved considerably by that point, and participating in conversations was more manageable, especially after a few glasses of wine.

The party lacked the Christmas spirit, the feeling of being surrounded by family or good friends, traditions, and especially snow. I hated not having snowy Christmas. It was the only winter holiday constant I hoped to keep from my childhood, from my past.

The evening started slow. We gathered at Lena's house early in the day to cook and set up for the party. Upon arrival, I jumped straight into the kitchen and started cooking while the rest decorated the room.

It was an open-plan kitchen and living room with the dining table conveniently placed between the cooking and sitting area. A big glass door conveyed access to the garden. After a couple of hours of preparation, we shifted into party mode, opening the first bottles of wine.

Adrian, accompanied by his son, arrived around 7 pm. We sat down to eat, sharing traditional Christmas foods from both countries, Romania and Poland.

I learned during this time how two brothers and two sisters got together, developing a symbiotic relationship of mutual benefit and, simultaneously, harm.

Adrian met Lena in Malta when she went to visit Suzanna for the first time. It wasn't love at first sight but more of a summer fling for her. As for Adrian, meeting Lena was a life-changing moment. He was recovering from a long and painful divorce, heartbroken by the love of his life. He found out about his wife's infidelity when, one day after finishing work earlier than usual, he went home to find her screwing his best friend. The pain and frustration caused by this incident drove him to despair, getting lost in his thoughts, always wondering where he went wrong and why this happened to him. Of course, we all have an opinion when something like this happens to someone, but I bet we all struggle with the same issues when it happens to us. I don't think that someone cheating results from a healthy relationship where communication intertwined with mutual respect stands at the foundation of partnership. From what I gathered, Adrian took his wife for granted, and she did what she had to do to supplement her needs and desires, to go out of a monotonous degrading relationship.

After two weeks of summer romance, Lena went back to the UK. Charmed by her looks and strong personality, Adrian packed his things and left Malta for good, leaving his son in the custody of his ex-wife. He needed more in his life and wanted to have the freedom to pursue the young love of a much younger girl. Lena didn't necessarily want him, but he was good to have around for a shag and a drive about her town. He fell madly in love with her and was driven once again to desperation when she did not want him.

And there we were all sat at the same table, with a dram of awkwardness lingering in the air.

Adding to the tension were Suzanna and Thom's constant disagreements that inevitably lead to a big argument towards the end of the evening. Their conversations always escalated into fights, but somehow they always met mid-ways by morning.

Through this entire heavily charged atmosphere, I stood still and quiet, downing glass after glass, waiting for the evening to end, which happened as expected: Carmen ignored me at all times except for the cold "I'm fine!" every time I enquired about her wellbeing; Adrian took his kid home before midnight leaving a drunken Lena sleeping in her bed; after a long fight at the end of the night, Thom went to sleep on the inflatable mattress in the living room while Suzanna slept with her sister leaving Carmen to slumber on the couch and me on an uncomfortable small armchair.

Christmas day started with a bang. Suzanna woke up with rashes all over her body, which led to her spending the whole day in the hospital with Lena and Thom by her side, while the rest of us spent the day cooking, eating, drinking, and entertaining the eight years old kid. Not much fun at all. From the moment I woke up that day, all I wanted was to go to the small moldy room in Walthamstow and sleep for as long as possible.

Unfortunately, Carmen's attitude towards me didn't change throughout the day, and I decided to stop asking her and let her come back to me when she realizes I did nothing wrong.

That late morning when Carmen and I were in the garden, shivering in the crisp winter air, smoking and drinking beer in the last attempt to recover from the previous night's agonous hangover, I asked her, breaking the pledge of silence to myself:

"Are you alright?" I asked, my voice broken with exhaustion. "I'm asking one last time, and I won't bother you again with this, I promise. It seemed you didn't have a good time last night."

"No, I'm not fucking alright!" Carmen replied astringently. "How the bloody hell was I supposed to enjoy myself last night when you started ignoring me the moment we walked through the fucking door?" Her chubby cheeks flushed with burning blood and anger; condensed spit started accumulating in the corners of her mouth.

"You know," she continued after a brief pause to slurp some beer from her third can, "I was very excited to be spending this Christmas with you, here in London, the place where our dreams were supposed to come true, but you've chosen to ignore me. Instead of being there for me, you've abandoned me on that shitty couch. So all that was left for me to do was watch you drunkenly dance with Lena and Suzanna. Are they more interesting than me? Are they your friends more than I am? You know they're not available, right?"

"What? No," I answered, overwhelmed with disbelief. "I was drunk and wanted to have some fun, which by the way, didn't happen. I wanted to shake off the dreariness from my shoulders, and I invited you to do the same. But you glued yourself to the couch and stayed there all night. You even went to sleep on the same spot."

"Yeah, right!" Carmen said, rolling her eyes. "You did that because you saw me there and felt sorry for me. And you know what? You better never do that again!"

"Feel sorry for you or invite you to have a good time?"

"Both. I don't need your pity. And your kind of fun isn't fun for me," she said, standing up, bumping the plastic table, spilling my beer.

That was the end of the conversation on this matter, and I was glad for it. I'm not good with confrontation or bringing any defensive arguments when under pressure.

The following day, after a coffee and a slice of stale Polish poppy seed cake, Carmen and I made our way home. Unfortunately, it was not quite home because no matter what we tried, that room was too dirty, foreign, and crowded for us to grow fond of it, get comfortable, and feel settled.

We spent the long journey home in total silence. I just followed her like a pup, knowing that she will get us safely to Walthamstow. As we approached our destination, she broke the silence by asking me if I wanted to get a bite at the food court in the shopping center and maybe catch a movie after. It was reliving hearing her speak, knowing this was the first step into forgiveness. Even though I never believed I did something wrong, in her eyes, I screwed up, and now she was bringing the peace offering in the shape of words.

I didn't want to fight with her or with anybody for that matter because I suck at it. However, I had no choice but to spend the following week in her company as we were both off for the winter holidays.

Not having anyone besides the gang we left behind, we entertained each other the best we could. To compensate for the illicit behavior I was accused of and bring back the good spirits for the both of us, I had to devise a plan of action that would keep Carmen and her fisty mind occupied: I was to say yes to whatever activity she proposed, be as cheerful as possible, disregard my feelings once more, and put my fake optimistic mask on. It was quite a good plan, and I did a great job, considering that after all the quality time spent together, we agreed on booking a three-day holiday to Dublin.

Four

We landed at Dublin Airport at 7 am on the last Friday of January. After figuring out the means of transport to the city center, we boarded the bus and set off. It was mild outside, the sun trying to push its way through the clouded sky. The air seemed fresher and warmer than the one we left behind at Luton Airport. It felt more like spring than winter, and I loved it.

The winter holiday combined with two weeks of work and the wet, cold weather that snuck inside my soul weighed me down, tiring me, and transformed my exaltation into exhaustion. However, my companion was excited by our arrival in the *most exciting city close to home*, as she portrayed it, and her happy energy boosted my mood a fraction.

After getting off the shuttle bus, we made our way through the streets of Dublin until we came next to the Liffey River. We walked alongside it until a narrow with its quirk outlines allured us in. It was impressive. Murals, graffiti, small shops, pubs, and restaurants shaped the streets with their looks, inviting you through a gateway to meet and feel the Irish spirit of the city.

Tired and hungry, we decided to stop for breakfast on the terrace of a pub on Dame Street. A cheerful waitress with an East European accent brought us the breakfast menu and asked if we would like to start with some hot beverages while deciding on the food order.

"Can we get two pints of lager and two cappuccinos, please?" said Carmen with a smile, awaiting a solid reaction to her order from our server's part.

"Don't wanna spoil your holiday, but we aren't allowed to serve alcohol before 10 pm. However, I can put the order through and bring it to you when possible. Is that ok?" said the server with a smile on her face while I buried my shame in the laminated pages of the food menu.

We received our coffees shortly after placing the order and had a smoke. Carmen went to the bathroom right after we agreed on the food order, leaving me alone at the table. While gazing in the distance along the road, watching people passing by in the morning sun, a muscly arm interrupted the movie rolling before my eyes. A tallish guy with brown hair and dark eyes brought two pints.

"Sorry to have startled you," he said in a croaky voice, "I thought you deserve a beer five minutes before ten. I noticed from behind the bar that you look tired, and a pint might brighten you and your experience here in Dublin. Sara, the waitress, told me you're tourists."

He spoke in a sweet and gentle Irish accent. My mouth opened slightly, involuntarily. I bathed my eyes in the image of this Adonis of a man standing in front of me, his shirt shyly concealing his sculpted body. His black jeans bulging in front of me invited my stare to fall upon his crotch and stay there.

"Oh. Thanks," I said, swallowing the excess saliva accumulated in my mouth. I smiled, not knowing what to say. My conversation skills were limited to friends and awkward jokes that don't make sense in English, so I decided to smile and avoid further embarrassment. Yes, I felt embarrassed for looking at him because I believed he might have noticed me studying him, head to toes.

I was brought out of awkwardness by Carmen's return. She sat down, giving him a quizzing look. I thanked him again for bringing the beers and moved my attention to Carmen. We cheered and greedily slurped our cold drinks.

The holiday has officially started, and we were there to enjoy it. After a big breakfast consisted of toast, eggs, sausages, and bacon, brought to us by Sara, we ordered one more pint. After that, we started planning our weekend in the Irish capital, slowly shifting the conversation towards the state of our friendship, each bringing up some facts we disliked about the other. She said about my alien presence and how much I changed towards her in the few months spent in London. I brought up her drinking problem to make her feel ashamed and avoid a conversation I dreaded having.

The second pint filled me up, so I headed for the toilet located on the establishment's first floor. While aiming for the stairs, I looked behind the bar to see the hunky man with the sexy voice one more time, but he wasn't there.

Guided by the intoxicating smell of chlorine, I entered a well-lit restroom, leaving the heavy wooden door slam with a bang behind me. To my delight, there he was. The enticing Adonis stood in front of the urinal, cock in hand, looking startled at me. I froze, my eyes dropping on his manhood, my brain rushing to process that image for my hand job material collection.

"Sorry about that," I said after the split second it took me to realize I should not look at men in a men's room and slid behind him and locked myself in a cubicle, not before noticing him smiling at me.

After I peed, I listened for any movement in the restroom. Then, to avoid him, I sat locked in the cubicle for a short while. I used the time to close my eyes and bring to the surface the image of him at the urinal. I could vividly see his, although flaccid, big dick and the forceful stream of urine that flowed out of his foreskin-covered knob — lip biting.

Exiting the stall, I checked my surroundings for any sign of life, then washed my hands and rushed through the bathroom door to get to Carmen as soon as possible. Unfortunately, I haven't seen the man standing right beside the staircase and almost collided with him in my hurry.

"Third time's a charm," his voice echoed in the empty dining room. "Hi. I'm Derek," he said, extending his arm inviting me to shake it.

"Hi…" said I in a shy voice, my cheeks catching fire. "I'm Thom."

The handshake lasted longer than the norm. It started strong from his side, a firm but gentle grasp which prolonged into him holding my hand. My palm sweated in response to his heat and ardor.

"Nice meeting you, Thom. Where are you from? Can't recognize your sweet accent."

"Romania… but traveling from London."

"Is the girl outside your girlfriend or, if I'm reading you right, just a friend?"

"She's my friend. Why are you…" I said, choking on my words and pulling my hand from his grasp. "Why do you ask? She seems attracted to you, so I can pass her a message if you're interested in her."

He chuckled at my words,

"No, silly. I'm interested in you," he paused to take in my reaction and said, "and was wondering maybe I can get your number? I want to ask you out for a drink. Maybe you can ditch her or something and let me show you the good side of Dublin tonight?"

"I'm… I'm sorry. I can't." Words struggled to leave my mouth. I was flattered and astonished by Derek's action. Never in my life had a man asked me out. My throat tightened, my heart skipped a beat, and I heard myself saying defensively: "I'm not… gay."

Derek smiled, and taking my hand, he placed a folded post-it in it, saying with a calm voice and somehow disappointed:

"This is my number in case you change your mind. I finish my shift at five." He squeezed my hand lightly, winked smilingly at me, and rushed downstairs, leaving me bewildered at the top.

I composed myself and followed him at a natural, unrushed pace. I walked past Derek, which was polishing a glass behind the bar, and avoided making eye contact with him. At the table, Carmen had already ordered another round of drinks. That beer was what I needed to recover from the rush of emotions I experienced on my journey to the loo.

We spent the subsequent few hours drinking, admiring the architecture of the buildings surrounding us, watching people passing by, and planning the day. It was once again lovely to spend time in her company, feeling our wrecked friendship starting to heal once more. I was pumped after my brief encounter with Derek, the Adonis, which helped with my confidence that I might have a chance in this world to meet someone, to fall in love. The alcohol helped too.

We set off to check-in at our hotel, which was just fifteen minutes walk from the pub. All we had planned for the rest of the afternoon was a nap and a shower, and we stuck with it. In the evening, we went for a walk on the busy streets of Dublin, growing fonder with the feel of the city. I had the same feeling there as I had the first time I set foot in London – I could see myself living there. Carmen suggested grabbing dinner at the same pub on Dean Street while listening to the live band playing that night. She might have pictured a romantic set-up for a night spent together, but I didn't. I agreed with dining there because I knew I would not see Derek as he had the night off.

I was quiet for most of the evening, pretending my attention was dedicated to the band, when in fact, staring at the stage, I drifted into imagining how my night might have looked like if, instead of Carmen, Adonis was sat in front of me. The daydreaming when as far as asking myself how would it feel to have walked the streets of Dublin holding Derek's hand, him showing me the secrets of the city, the non-touristic side of it. How we might have kissed in the shade of a statue or a corner of an alley. How he would insist on me going to his place and initiate me in the sins of the flesh. What might have been if I would have been honest with myself and others.

The next day after breakfast, we set off to discover the treasures that Dublin held. Carmen purchased a city tour on one of those hop-on-hop-off busses, which took us around throughout the day. We made a couple of hours detour from the usual route and visited Glasnevin Cemetery, founded in 1832. Carmen had a thing for old cemeteries, so I complied and followed her lead. We read the tombstones and searched for famous people buried there, took pictures of intricately designed sculptures that adorned the graves of the unknowns, and stood quietly in the sad shadows of the Angels Plot. In this place, stillborn babies rested on consecrated ground.

In the evening, we went back to the pub on Dean Street for a nightcap where I saw my Adonis, Derek, the barkeep, for the last time. I don't think he spotted me in the crowd, but I watched him briefly from a corner, wished him all the best without a word, and thanked him for making me feel wanted and beautiful enough to attract a man's attention. He gave me the confidence I lacked my entire life, a good sense of self-appreciation I thought I'll never have.

We arrived in our bleak room in sunny Walthamstow that Sunday afternoon and fell back in our routine form the following day. I saved Derek's number with the hope and promised that one day when I'd be ready to be myself, I would drop him a text.

Five

The spring arrived with the usual fuss of nature and brought with it the freedoms of the soul. Once incarcerated in the depressions of the gloomy winter days, we were once more optimistic regarding our future.

Carmen and I were in a perfect place in our friendship. Once more, we were confiding in each other – she more than I, me keeping my secret was still the number one priority – and the routine of work and spending time together whenever she had the weekend off brought back her hope, rekindling the love she had for me. On the other side, with a cold heart, I pretended not to notice her flirt.

In late March, Suzanna and Thom came to visit us in Walthamstow. We couldn't accommodate them in our beautifully infested lodgings, so we arranged to take them to the pub up the road. It was nice to have made some friends by coincidence. We missed having someone to spend time with as much as they did, so that was perfect for all of us. Carmen had one more friend, the one that helped her get the job, while I had just the reminiscences of my past Romanian life.

We met them in front of the pub. Located in the front of a junction, the establishment was popular amongst locals that served as décor every time we went there for a burger and a drink. The carpeted floors preserved the musty, sour smell of the years gone by; the sticky tables bore the names and affairs of those that passed through, and the not-so-friendly staff looked like they've witnessed the erection of the building back in the 1800s. The food was the usual frozen, premade stuff you get in low-class establishments. It was cheap. The beer was on tap. What more could we ask for in our "I'm gonna make it in London" penniless situation? But, that was the local, and we enjoyed it so much that we took our guests there.

The evenings were still cold, so we sat at a table inside. Thom and I brought the drinks while Carmen and Suzanna started the gossip at the table.

After we all stated how we've been in the past week, the reason for their visit surfaced. A double room was to be available from mid-April in their shared house, and they thought that all of us living together would be a great idea. And it sounded like one. The thrill we felt was indescribable, and we agreed to go the next day to see the room.

The excitement lasted for longer than expected, which affected my sleep. So on that Saturday, I woke up before Carmen and headed to the coffee shop at the rear of William Morris Gallery for lattes and pastries. I woke up my friend with freshly brewed coffee and dragged her out of bed to get ready to go and see our new potential home in Peckham.

Traveling by bus from Elephant and Castle Underground Station to meet Thom, we had a chance to take in the neighborhood's look and vibe. It appeared messy, chaotic, and noisy with a hint of unsafeness. I wasn't particularly pleased with what I saw, and neither was Carmen. She has been quiet throughout our journey there and, while sat on the upper deck of the 172 bus, I realized how less we talked lately when we were alone. It felt as if we knew each other so well that the small talk was unjustified, confirming my need to be closer to other people, other friends, so I prayed for the house we were about to see to be better than the rubbish pit we were living in.

A fresh-looking Thom was waiting for us at the bus stop. He was a freelance barista which allowed him to schedule his working days as he pleased, and by doing so, he went to work just when money was low. Thom was waiting for that big break in his life when he would jump at the opportunity of creating something great that would bring with it fame and recognition. For me, he looked like an accomplished intellectual with great ideas and potential, for whom the universe will give everything with no effort on his part.

"Hello! And welcome to the neighborhood," he greeted us cheerfully as we got off the bus. "What has happened to you? You lot look hangover," he grinned while opening his tote bag unveiling a load of canned Romanian beers, "and am glad I've got some hair of the dog to bring your spirits up."

"I'm dying for a beer!" Carmen exclaimed enthusiastically while I refrained from joining in the conversation, feeling queasy at the thought of drinking again.

We crossed the road with Thom leading the way and stopped in front of a dusty grey door right across the street from the bus stop. Unlocking the door, he invited us in. Leaving behind the noisy street adorned with bin bags and dirt, we walked in a poorly lit, tall, and narrow hallway that led to a staircase. A few seconds later, I adjusted to the murky interior once the door was shut behind us, leaving the kitchen door at the top of the stairs the only source of light. Quietly and full of hope, we followed our host on the first landing, where he showed us a well-lit, clean, and small kitchen. A counter and two bar stools served the porpoise of a dining table; two fridges were neatly shoved in the remaining space between the fire escape door and the sink; an array of cupboards and drawers embellished the remaining space providing enough storage for all the tenants. It looked well designed and suitably equipped – and small at the same time - for nine people.

Our potential double room was located on the top floor of the building with just another single room on the same landing, with easy access to the roof terrace. Polished wooden floors made it look authentic; the bed was double and considerably more significant than the one we were sharing in our Walthamstow furry cave. An ample wardrobe provided enough space for Carmen to put all her clothes in, and the desk completed the room's furniture nicely. We were sold. After agreeing to take on the room even if the rent cost was almost double in price, we sat down on the terrace and enjoyed few beers in the spring sun.

In April, we moved.

Flustered and excited, we rearranged the furniture to suit our style and cleaned every corner before unpacking the suitcases. The roof terrace became our living room. Carmen was happy. I was content. For me, the pros of us moving into the new place were obvious: I was closer to Thom and Suzanna; my journey to work reduced from more than an hour on public transport to a mere seven-minute walk; the bed was big, which meant more space between my pal and me; the kitchen was clean, so I could stop eating junk food and start cooking. I had only one point on the cons side of the list: I was still living with Carmen, and this was about to change.

The following months came and went without notice. A well-established routine settled: work Monday to Friday, big shopping for food on Saturday, and finishing the weekend with lengthy stays on the roof, drinking. Carmen and I rarely met due to her hectic work schedule, which was fine by me. I had some more privacy in my room, some time for myself to wank, cry, or dream of a more unburdened life for me.

However, I felt incarcerated in my own life by my mind, which slowly chipped at my self-esteem and happiness. The more I tried to hide my feeling under the cheerful, always smiling mask I've put on every morning, the more I felt as the world needed to stop for me so I could catch a break, so I could breathe. Life in London wasn't what I envisioned, and I was disappointed. I wanted to make a change, start, and build that incredible dream I always had, but nothing was closely and safely available to me without crushing Carmen's heart, tearing us apart.

In mid-July, after my birthday, Carmen came home from work upset and angrier than ever before. It was a sunny Saturday afternoon, and I was sat reading on the roof. She opened the terrace door forcefully and pushed it closed with her foot with a power that startled me.

"You alright?" I said, closing my book and placing it on the table.

"Alright… my ass," she replied, throwing herself on the plastic chair opposite me. She pulled out a cigarette and lit it, inhaling deeply. "I'm fucked. Absolutely FUCKED!" she shouted, making me cringe a little in my seat.

Carmen wasn't the one to share her life easily. She always tended to keep everything in and dissect it until nothing was left of it or the mess became so great that the only way to clean it was to throw it into someone else's life. She went over her mistakes and bad decisions by blaming others. My not-so-fair lady was about to explode like Vesuvius, and I was Pompeii.

"I'm about to lose my job," Carmen said with a broken voice. She composed herself, moving sharply in her chair, and then looked me deeply in the eyes. "This is unfair, and I'm in this position because of you!" she exclaimed, spatting on the table between us.

41

"What? How? My fault for…" I was speechless, confused, and shocked at her words. I knew from her how much she hated her waitress job at the private club and how much she enjoyed the people and the parties they had behind the scenes during work. She always came home half-drunk, but none of this was my fault. I haven't made her drink or disobey her superiors. I didn't even work there.

"Don't play stupid," she barked at me. "You drove me to desperation with your behavior, allure, and ignorance. I am tired of you and of what you made me become. And now, I'm going to lose everything because of you, and I hate you and blame you for it!" Her face was red like hot iron, and droplets of foam started forming in the corners of her mouth. She was shouting, which made me grow small in my seat, trying to shield myself from her poisonous words.

She conveyed a monolog in which she was the victim and I, Thomas O'Lorr, the assailant. Carmen's words delivered with force and fire exposed her carefully sheltered frustrations and feelings towards me, who piled up throughout the year.

She started from the beginning, from when we first met at the small restaurant back in Transylvania, and how she knew I was going to change her life forever from the moment she saw me. How nice of a guy I seamed from the beginning how trustworthy and grounded I appeared. Carmen then went on describing how much she trusted me and the excitement she had when I agreed to take our lives in our own hands and move to London to build a better life for ourselves and how much she sacrificed for me to succeed in this adventure, to find a place to live, to find a job and be happy and accomplished.

I agreed with her about how supportive she was and how much her generosity and altruism meant to me and helped me be where I was now. But getting a job at which I'm good at and seen as an accomplished and successful pastry chef has nothing to do with her. I'm where I am in my career due to sleepless nights of studying, discipline, burnt hands, and hard work in front of the stove and not due to her charity. I'm who I am due to my decisions and work, and I won't let her take credit for it. Unfortunately, she was too fired up, and I decided it wasn't a good time for me to disrupt her speech, so I stood there, small and wounded, listening to her.

Carmen was unstoppable, especially when she drank, so she described who she thought I was and what she envisioned our life in England would look like.

"I believed in you and your aptitudes when no one else did. I supported and guided your decisions to ensure your success…". She pulled another cigarette from the pack and lit it. I stood silent.

"And you? What have you done for me in the past year? Nothing! Your selfishness and arrogance will destroy you one day! All I'm saying is that I loved you, but you were too full of yourself to realize what you had right in front of you… right in your bed! A man like you will die alone!"

She shouted from across the table when I suddenly realized all of our flatmates could hear her. I was glad she spoke Romanian and that only Thom could understand what the fight was about – which he did. Thom, Suzanna, and two other tenants, disturbed and intrigued by the noise, sat quietly on the fire exit and listened to us arguing – Thom translating every word for those interested.

Realizing I wasn't about to answer any of her questions, Carmen jumped sharply to her feet, pushing the table towards me spilling my beer in my lap. I assume she got inspired by it and grabbed her can and threw it at me, hitting me in the face.

She left instantly, leaving me with my face in my palms, trying to stop myself from crying. Her words, "a man like you will die alone" fell as heavy as a millstone on my chest. My lifelong fear crippled me: never find love and die alone, not feeling how it is to love someone truly. And that bloody half-full beer can hit me in the nose, making it bleed.

From that day on, my relationship with Carmen degraded even more. Suzanna and Thom were very comprehensive of my situation and were very attentive when it came to support and entertainment. We became closer than ever, and on the bright side of things, they became my closest friends.

Carmen bonded with our next-door neighbor, a 36 years old vet from Hungary. They started the adventure of her life by going out clubbing and spending the little money she had. As towards me, Carmen was polite in our encounters – we were still sharing a bed at the end of the day - just enough not to spark another fight. She indeed lost her job a week later after our battle, and it wasn't funny. I vouched to myself that I would return the favors and support her as much as possible, and I did so. But she wouldn't let me. I tried to tell her how important it is for her to focus on finding another job, that I would take care of the rent for the foreseeable future. She refused my help to such extent that she went and borrowed money from a pawn shop at an incredibly high rate to prove her independence from me. To this day, I considered her actions stupid, but if our places would have been reversed, I, most probably, would have done the same.

I was frustrated with my living arrangements, and having Carmen home 24/7 drinking and wasting time wasn't of help for me and my sanity. I bet she cringed every time she saw me coming home from work too. I needed to spend more time outside the house and avoid unnecessary contact with her. The tension between us was so thick you could slice it with a sword.

As the August month stumbled upon us, Thom approached me while I was in one of my meditational escapades - sat on the terrace with a beer listening to music. I love music, and I love even more how much a random song can fit my soul like a glove in times of need. At that time, *Rise up* by Andra Day was on repeat.

"I have a brilliant idea, and I think you'll like it." Thom said, surrounded by his golden happy aura.

"Please, do tell!" I replied, pausing the song.

"I've discussed with Suzanna and did some research on the matter, and I found a flat that we could rent. It's at a reasonable price, and you would have your room, a living room, and a beautiful terrace... and no Carmen." He chuckled.

"Wow!" I said, feeling my heart skip a beat. "Where? When? How? How much?"

Thom laughed and presented me with the plan. The flat was one of four in a post-war building, split into two levels. The first floor housed the bedrooms and the bathroom. In contrast, the second level was composed of an open plan kitchen and living space – leading onto a beautiful roof terrace overlooking the entire neighborhood – plus a service toilet and plenty of storage on the hallway. He produced some pictures from his photo gallery on his phone, and frankly, ten minutes later, I was sold. It looked so good and the idea of me having my room and sharing a house with them, my two friends, was everything that I needed. It just felt right for this to be my next step, to detach myself from the negativity and tension surrounding me at that moment.

A week later, after providing the documentation and all the necessary information to the agency, they announced that we were eligible to rent, and so we paid the deposit. In all this time, it never occurred to me how I would deliver the news to Carmen and how she would feel. The day we got our approval, my anxiety engulfed me. I started, like any other overthinker – you might know how that goes – to wonder how to do it, developing scenarios and strategies and coming up with the same result.

When Albert Einstein said that "Insanity is doing the same thing over and over again expecting different results.", I think he also had in mind the overthinkers. As a result, I was sure I was driving myself insane by just waiting to find a way to spill the beans.

Two weeks before moving into my new home, I went on the terrace to find Carmen enjoying a beer alone. My chest cavity was smaller than a dime compressing my rapidly beating heart and lungs like a wreck in a car crusher on a junkyard.

"Hello there. How are you? Can we speak for a moment?" I said, placing a cold beer can on the table in front of her.

"Yeah. What's up again?" she said bitterly.

"You know how our lives went on different paths the moment you blamed me for your misfortunes," she grinned upon hearing my words, but I continued with a slight increase in volume, stopping her from saying anything, "and I think it is time for us to part ways. But listen to what I have to say first, and don't interrupt me. I found a place where to move... well, Thom did. And I tried to figure out a way to make our inevitable separation easier for both of us."

"Leave, and I'll figure it out myself. I don't need anything from someone like you!" said Carmen while hot flushes painted her face an angry red.

"Hey! Please don't shout. I want to have a normal conversation so we can figure it out together. So please listen to me for a second."

She stopped, leaned back in her chair, and listened to me while smoking nonchalantly. I presented her the only way I saw we could have done this with minimal discomfort. First, I was to pay my share of rent for the following two months so she can have the time to arrange something for herself in the meantime. Second, I was to leave the room and move out on the 1st of September, giving her space and time to figure out her next step. I apologized for my decision and told her I felt like I was abandoning her, but at the same time, it felt right to move forward. Carmen agreed with my plan and promised to give me back the rent money after she finds a job and sorts out her life – she never did, and I never expected her to do so.

On the 1st of September, after carrying my bags to Adrian's car, I said my farewell to Carmen. It felt strange. The tension between us had vanished, and all that was left there for us were the good memories and the realization that I wouldn't have been there at that exact moment if it wasn't for her. I gave her a long and tight hug and whispered in her ear:

"Thank you. I wish you all the best, and please don't hesitate to ask for help if you need it. You know where to find me. Thank you again, and best of luck!"

Carmen kissed me on the chicks and wished me the best of luck while I turned my back to her and headed for the door. That was the last time I saw her, and to this day, I'm grateful for her being part of my life, even if it was for a short time and her words "a man like you will die alone" still haunt me.

Six

A year after the traumatic experience of starting a life from scratch in a new country, a new city, and with limited resources, my life started getting the shape I wanted it to be. It was still raw and uncertain, like a fragile seedling bursting out of the ground looking for the warming rays of the spring sun. The new home, plus my new flatmates, were the exact things I needed to ease the twisted rope of secrets around my neck. I felt at ease for a short time with myself. I had the privacy of my personal space, two friends that started considering me their adopted son, and a place I felt I could call it home. One might not realize how important it is to think that one belongs to a place. So far in my adventure, I ignored and declined the need to do and feel as such for the benefit of others, but now that I've done it, it felt good.

After spending a year in two unwelcoming places, Walthamstow and at the border of Peckham with Bermondsey, Putney was a massive improvement, in my opinion, regarding the location, the look, and feel of a London neighborhood. Our flat was on Felsham Road, in a quiet residential area just a few minutes walk from the main street and the riverside.

Upon arrival at our new house, we set up the main rules of cohabitation - we were to share everything and make the new place the best home we could have. We were three people with different views and tastes, which somehow intertwined to create a sanctuary from the mad world outside. It was what a home should be.

Unconsciously each of us settled in our routines. My company opened a new production kitchen in Islington and relocated my pastry section there. Luckily my two funny and close colleagues were relocated too: Lala, a forty years old, single, red-headed Bulgarian woman, and Jakub, a twenty-five years old gay lad from Poland. The team was small, which facilitated the development of a long-lasting friendship with them, resulting in notorious Friday drinks after work, reliability, and trust between us. The evenings were composed of a home-cooked dinner with my adoptive parents, Thom and Suzanna, followed by drinks on the terrace or a movie. The weekends became monotonous too: brunch at home Saturday and Sunday, the weekly cleaning of the flat on one of the days, and mainly no social activities afterward. The exceptional case was when a dinner party was organized by one of us. In this way, we started creating a more extensive social group. My friends became theirs and vice-versa.

As the weeks rolled on into December, I grew more and more anxious about the upcoming of another Christmas in London. Then, finally, Thomas and Suzanna decided to go to Poland and spend the holidays with Suzanna's family, while all the other friends I had already made plans that weren't involving me. In a way, this was what I wanted. For the first time in my life, I could spend Christmas and New Year's Eve alone, just me, food, drinks, and a dildo. Two whole weeks of being home alone didn't sound bad.

I wrapped up work for the year on the 22nd of December and would return on the 2nd of January. After finishing the day around midday, I headed to a sex shop near Earls Court – after doing some research on this type of shop. From the street, the only thing that gave up the store's content was a small shop window in which mannequins were sporting leather straps and some fancy underwear. I paced up and down the street, smoking and trying to build the courage to enter. I knew I wanted to, but less we forget I was still a closeted gay man. I kept on telling myself that no one would recognize me, that I should take advantage of the anonymity provided by living in a metropolis. Finally, after stubbing out my cigarette, I took a deep breath and adjusted my voice to seem confident. I pushed open the door to make sure I entered as quickly as possible but not too fast to attract attention or divulge my emotions.

The door opened into a short, small hallway that resembled a photo booth, designed to prevent the passers-by from seeing the glory of the interior and provided privacy to the shoppers. On the speakers, generic electronic music played at a decent volume and, combined with the room's lighting, transcended me into a beautiful universe. An array of jockstraps, gay magazines, lubes, poppers, dildos, flashlights, cock accessories, and other stuff I have never seen in my life were neatly arranged and displayed on the walls, shelves, and counters. It was freaking heaven. I felt like a kid in a candy store. What candy store?! It was a fucking Willy Wanking Factory, if you may, and I loved it!

At the till, a young man with pink dyed hair, tattoos on both arms, neck, and face, and some prominent thick piercings welcomed me and offered his assistance. I politely declined and told him I was watching but will ask for his help if needed. I smiled at him, and he returned the gesture. After that, all I wondered was what he would think of me when I would head to the counter with a cock in my hand. Oh, the self-destroying mentality of caring for other people's opinions.

I made my way around the shop, looking for the dildo section. I founded shortly and discovered that the selection from their website was considerably smaller than the one in store. I was glad for being the only customer in there, considering it was the Christmas shopping season. This allowed me to take in and check all the sizes and variations of the products. I picked up the ones that looked like something I would enjoy and read the descriptions looking at length, girth, and other specifications. I knew I was a bottom and, as presented in the shop, men came in different sizes and shapes, and I didn't want to buy a toy that would stretch my whole at a level at which it would be hard to find a partner that could satisfy me and in reverse, for me not to be too loose to please him. The realization of me needing to concern myself with not just my penis but with others' hit me right there in the shop. What a life I signed up for.

I chose an eight-inch dildo with a thick shaft and suction cup, priced at almost £100. It seemed expensive, but I thought of it as a Christmas present to myself and an investment considering that now I had a room in which no one would enter without my approval, so hiding it from everyone was easy.

I paid, and after the embarrassing "Have a great Christmas!" followed by a wink and a smile from the till guy, I headed home with my new toy stuffed in my backpack. I shivered with anticipation and could not wait for the second day to wake up in an empty house and try it.

The evening of that day consisted of a nice dinner and a bottle of red wine with Thom and Suzanna, followed by an exchange of presents. I got an electric razor for him – thinking of the places I used mine and the places Thom used it when he borrowed it – and a professional hair-dryer for Suzanna, knowing that hers was on its way out. In return, they gifted me a set of Happy Socks, my favorite, and a nice hipsterish tie. Little did they know they have given me more than that: a holiday of self-satisfaction with my fabulous new toy!

The morning came with much-expected anticipation. I woke up early to an empty flat. My flatmates left the house in the middle of the night, and so I started preparing for what was to be a full day of fucking. With the help of my morning coffee, the first bowel movement came with no trouble, and I followed it with a deep cleansing of my intestines. This time I have completed the research on how to do an enema for a better and successful anal play. It took time and patience to prepare myself, but I wanted to avoid the unfortunate situation of shitting all around the house as I did in that hotel room.

I headed to the store to grab some food supplies and water-based lube in the relaxation and readjustment period between pushing water up my ass and the safe anal penetration. I was planning on not going out for the following few days. Just sit around, enjoy myself, and release the sexual tension and frustration accumulated over the past months. And so I did — three days of anal play and a carousel of gay porn.

If you ask me how I felt, well, it felt amazing, but all of it was a bit too much. I was physically exhausted, my muscles were tense and flooded with lactic acid, and my pussy was sore like hell. But it was worth feeding the beast inside of me.

On New Year's Eve, I made myself a pizza, opened a bottle of Prosecco, and binge-watched an old-time favorite sitcom *Two Broke Girls* – the funny story of two girls from different backgrounds met and became friends and business partners trying to make a better life for themselves - when, in one of the episodes, Max, the pessimist, a dark-humored character I identified with uses a hook-up app to attract gay men to their cupcake shop, by pretending to be a hunk Latino man. I have never heard of that phone app before, and at first, I thought it was just the creation of the writers to convey a series of funny jokes. But, shortly after, I found myself searching for it. When the download was complete, I created a profile on that app.

When my profile was uploaded, and the interface came to life, I felt the same surge of adrenaline and endorphins as I felt in the sex shop a few days earlier. I couldn't believe my eyes: an array of profiles with or without pictures, with faces or just torsos, legs, or screenshots of conversations; lengthy description of individuals and their sexual preferences; profiles categorized by sexual position, descriptive labels; and their distance from my device. It looked like a box of chocolates waiting for me to indulge its content.

I wasn't the one to text or bothered people with any likes; I just stayed low and watched who was around. Constantly fearing to have my greatest secret uncovered and not knowing who else might be secretly gay from those few people I knew, I kept my profile picture a default blank, and as a name, I just posted *T*. I thought someone would want to chat with me if I stayed online, and so I did. In all this time, I could feel drops of pre-cum forming on the knob of my penis and slowly making their way out from underneath the foreskin onto my underwear, making me feel wet and sticky. I started fantasizing about meeting some of the guys created scenarios on how I would do it and where.

It was around 9 pm when I decided to go and clean my rectum. I wanted to be prepared in case the app would have the best of me by the end of the night, and I would give in and meet someone. So I left my phone upstairs while thoroughly cleaning my pussy. This took me about an hour. To my surprise, three men texted me in that time. The first one was a twenty-four years old chubby cub. His message was short: *Hey! What are you up to?* It was followed by three pictures with him from the waist up, no shirt on. He went by the name of *ChubbyTop*.

The second message came from a blank profile; the only description displayed *just looking*. He texted: *Hello neighbor! New to this app? Are you into older guys? Daddy type here.*

The third text came from a guy with a huge penis and a muscular body, located within a five-mile radius. It's all I can say about him because at the moment I opened his message and saw the picture of him naked on the bed with his fully erected monster, I instantly went hard, panicked, and had no idea how to reply.

It seemed that everyone had some nude pictures to share in the private chat, so I had to have some to succeed on the app. So I took my clothes off and tried my best to take pretty pictures of my cock, my ass, my hole, and a more unpleasant one of my whole wiggly body. I had people telling me I wasn't that fat, but I knew better, and I was disgusted, but I thought I could share this with those who are very interested and keen to meet, just to scare them away.

I went back on the app after editing the photos, and the first thing I did was send a pic of my pussy to the monster dick man. It wasn't a surprise when he blocked me.

ChubbyTop wasn't my type. I had daddy issues, and I was a bottom in need of an experienced man. So I replied to his inquiry shortly, saying I wasn't up to too much and was planning on calling it a day and head to sleep, and after I went on and texted The Daddy.

Hello, neighbor! I typed, trying to steal some time to come up with the perfect reply, but miserably failed at it. *How are you? Yes, I am new to this app. Just found out about it and went for it. Haha.*

Him: *Nice. You'll find here whatever your heart desires. Welcome to the SINNER'S CLUB!*

Me: *Thanks. What are you up to?*
Him: *Do you like mature men?*
Me: *Yes.*
Him: *Well, you're in luck! I'm a daddy and not just only by name.*

Me: *What do you mean?*
Him: *HaHa! Don't be scared. I'm a father… and I'm married.*

His text took me by surprise! I was shocked. I used to think that maybe one day, if I stayed in Romania and complied with the unwritten laws of my community, I would have to marry and have kids to protect my secrets and appearances. But, I couldn't help but wondered why a gay man would do such a thing here, in London, where people from all around the world come, connect and learn to tolerate, appreciate or accept everyone, where the city's population is so extensive and diverse that everyone has his place if they look for it. I haven't found mine yet but was looking for it.

I shook my head to rid myself of these judgmental thoughts and told myself that everyone is entitled to his story, and we all have our motives and beliefs upon which we act and make our decisions. It wasn't my place to judge.

I believe my long pause in replying to his text made him redirect the conversation, and he sent me a picture of his body taken from his chest towards his feet, lying on his bed showcasing a flat and somehow muscular abdomen, with just a touch of hairy. The main focus of the image was his perfect-looking manhood. It looked just right: thick enough, long enough, and with a beautiful wet and pinkish head shining in the artificial light of his room. Upon seeing it, a cold shiver shot down my spine straight to my cock, my hair stood on ends, and my butthole clenched. He was so hot I couldn't help it, so I placed two fingers in my mouth, licked them, and scooped some saliva. Then, spreading my legs, I started playing with my pussy.

His picture was shortly followed by him asking me if I like what I saw, to which I replied with a set of three photos of me playing with my hot, wet hairy whole. I told him I loved it, to which he said, after seeing my pictures, that my pussy was made for his cock, and if we are not to be careful, I might get pregnant. Placing my phone down next to me, I grabbed my hard dick and stroke it hard while vigorously abusing my hole with my fingers. Hot loads of sperm exploded on my hairy chest, making me shrunk and quiver on the small couch in the living room. The image of him fucking me stood with me for a few more seconds. Finally, I picked up the phone, snapped a picture of the mess I was in, and sent it to him with the caption, "If you made me do this to myself with just one pic, I can't imagine what it would be like actually to have you inside me…." And he was gone. He signed-out.

I was disappointed for not reconnecting with him that evening, but I assumed his wife must have been around. So I closed the app and went to bed.

Seven

The spring had arrived that year slower than usual. Some rainy and dark days prolonged the depressive state I prolapsed in at the beginning of the year. I realized later how toxic it was not to be ready to put myself out there and jump headfirst in a shark-infested pool and wait for someone to bite and take me out of my misery.

After my New Year's Eve experience, I kept the app on but didn't show my face on it. My crack, cock, and chubby body were there for anyone that sent me nudes to see. I came across some good-looking guys and some not-so-good-looking ones, but in the end, we all have a type, right? The men I liked were never interested in me, or maybe they ignored me because I kept my face hidden. Or that my sole reason for the app was to collect as many nudes as possible? Who knows.

I was sad. I felt so lonely and unwanted. Everything good that happened to me passed by like a train in an empty station. At that time, I couldn't realize what went wrong with me, how my perfect plan went sloughed off my vision board and vanished. So, I took on long walks in the rain by the riverside, listening to Adele, soul-searching, trying to figure out what's the porpoise of all the things that were happening to me. I needed to see the cause to understand the effect, desperately grasping at straws to keep myself from sinking, trying to stay in abeyance over my life. I felt as the end was near for me, the darkness engulfing, bit by bit, my mind and soul. And so, one night during one of my walks, I wiped off my tears and decided to go for it, to be myself and not caring about others' opinions and concerns, that besides my life, I had nothing to lose.

I went home and, lying on my bed, uploaded a picture of me on my hook-up app profile. I went as far as creating a Tinder account. And thus, a new chapter of my life began.

It is hard to connect with those you speak with online, the tone set in a virtual environment can be dispassionate and frugal. One of my first Tinder matches was Richard, a 28 years old museum curator from London. He was keen on establishing a connection and developed a conversation that shortly after we connected, we exchanged numbers and took the conversation off the app.

During a week of constant chat and picture swaps, he asked me out. He was good-looking, not my Irish Adonis, but cute. He had short hair, balding - as far as I saw in his pictures - blue eyes and a cheeky smile. So I agreed to meet him for a beer near South Kensington Station.

We set a date for the following Friday evening. I wanted to take my time and stop by my flat after work to shower and change, to make myself more comfortable in my skin. I was flushed with emotions that day, and any minor inconvenience could have kept me from going. He worked in that area and being in the known I left him to decide the meeting place.

The pub was located just across the station, a classic British one in all its glory. Unfortunately, by the time I arrived at the location, I was sweaty and shaky and could barely contain myself. This date felt like entering a haunted forest where birds ate the breadcrumbs, costing me finding my way out of it.

I walked into the pub, ordered a pint, and went outside to calm my nerves and smoke a cigarette. After almost chucking the beer down my throat, I saw him. Richard walked out of the establishment with a beer in his hand, smiling and looking insistently at me. He was dressed in a black shirt with a small yellow floral print, black jeans, and a navy suit jacket. I instantly realized he was taller than I expected and not as cute as I imagined him to be. We shook hands while introducing each other and went to sit down at one of the tables on the makeshift terrace. The conversation went smoothly on his side. As for mine, let's say that I wasn't accustomed to understanding a cockney accent. I felt stupid for being able to understand just half the words he said. To make it work, I devised a questionnaire that will mostly keep him talk while I would nod and smile. It worked for the first hour of our date. Then he started asking me questions regarding my upbringing, Romania, how I like it in London, about work, friends, and started debating my irrational disgust of fish and seafood. Thankfully, I was drunk by that point and couldn't care less if my accent was too strong or if he would get offended if I consistently asked him to repeat his sentences or explain any references he made. The tension and shakiness had disappeared, and I fully relaxed and stopped pretending I was someone I wasn't.

Shortly after eight o'clock, he told me he had made reservations to his favorite Italian restaurant, which was a ten-minute walk from the pub.

"Is it alright if I hold your hand?" Richard asked me as we walked down Cromwell Road.

"Yes," I said with a tremble in my voice and offered him my opened palm.

We arrived at the restaurant, where the hostess led us to a table outside. He ordered a bottle of rose for both of us and a portion of tuna pasta for him, which I thought was the most disgusting item on the menu considering it was fish. I never understood how one could enjoy canned tuna. For me, it was the worst invention of humanity, next to the atomic bomb and sushi. I had the vegetarian pesto pasta.

We ate in silence, intending to stuff ourselves as quickly as possible to satisfy the hunger that possessed us.

The wine was good but sweet for my taste, and the smell of tuna made me gag a few times, but I controlled my outbursts with a smile. After splitting the bill, Richard invited me for a nightcap at a pub near the museum. I agreed and went to have a gin and tonic even if my system wasn't capable of assimilating any alcohol by that point. I felt drunk, and walking became a tad difficult. Thankfully I had him to lean on under the pretext of holding hands. On our way to the new location, he stopped abruptly in the middle of the sidewalk, grabbed me tightly by the waist with one arm while the other found its way on the back of my neck, and kissed me passionately. At first, his wet lips met mine with force, but he gently opened his mouth and pushed his tongue in my mouth. I resisted briefly to this invading force, but I gave in in the end and kissed him back. He was a good kisser, but the taste of tuna still lingering in his mouth turned my stomach upside down. I braked off his embrace to catch a breath and contain the mini vomit that was making its way up inside my mouth. I swallowed whatever churned pesto pasta invaded the back of my throat and said with a smile:

"Wow! I wasn't expected that. I'm so drunk my senses are paralyzed. I wanted to be much more prepared for this."

"I'm sorry, but I couldn't contain the desire to kiss you any longer," he said with a grin.

"Oh, don't get me wrong, please. I just wanted to be prepared and take a mint before kissing you. It makes me feel more comfortable knowing you won't taste my bitter beer and garlic breath." I laughed, and taking out a mint, offered one to him too, with the hope he would take it and kill the stench of his mouth. Thank God, and to all Saints that he did. I could now succumb to his desires and my first date with a man.

We arrived at the pub, where I went straight to the loos. The vast amount of beer was taking over my bladder. I stood in front of the urinal, analyzing the kiss and his actions that evening, and concluded that I liked him but should be more careful with where we get intimate due to my fear of being seen.

Pushing my way through the crowded pub, I met him at the bar. He offered to pay for my drink, and while we waited for the bartender to serve us, I noticed a group of three young guys looking our way. Paranoid as I was, I panicked, but after a scrutinizing look around, I saw Richard making a thumb up sign and realized he knew them. It seemed weird that he had friends around, and I thought he might have told them he would meet me that day, and they came to check me out. It was cute in a way but creepy.

Sat outside in a darker corner of the terrace, we smoked and drank and fooled around, kissing and hugging. I mainly stood in Richard's arms, where I started acknowledging how great it can be to let go of my fears and let myself be loved by someone – and also needed the support to stay straight. At one point, I noticed his friends sitting and watching us from the opposite corner and panicked. I checked the time and told him it was late and that I would like to go home. He agreed, and we downed our drinks.

Halfway to the station, we stopped on a poorly lit part of the street and kissed. Richard gently moved one hand from my neck and, after stroking my back, placed it on my ass. He grabbed my butt cheek and squeezed it hard. I quivered with pleasure. He smiled, his blue eyes flickering in the dim street light. I kissed him more while he forced his hand inside my pants, pressing his middle finger on my sphincter. A rush of electric impulses took over my senses and made my cock harden. With his other hand, he guided my right palm to his crotch, indicating to stroke him. I clumsily tried to undo his belt for easy access. He noticed my inability, so he helped, going a step further and unbuttoned his jeans.

I was aroused and wanted more. I pulled Richard's hand out of my trousers, licked his fingers, ensuring a good amount of saliva covered them - to facilitate an easy penetration, and whispered to him to stick them inside me. He obliged. I moaned in ecstasy when the top of his thick finger pushed its way in and, with increasing force, massaged and puled at my hole.

I placed my hand inside his pants and found a nice erect cock throbbing, pre-cum covering my fingers and palm. I grabbed it and started stroking it, kissing him intensely. He then pushed me in the obscurity of an entrance door of a building, out of the view of passing cars. Pinning me to the wall, he pressed his pelvis on my belly, trapping my hand with his dick in it between us, and started thrusting, making his foreskin move up and down his knob. In contrast, with his hands, he pulled my trousers down just enough to expose my ass, spread my cheeks, and pushed to fingers inside my already wet whole. Minutes later, he came in my hand. Richard looked at me in delight and pulled himself off me.

"That was a first for me."

"For me too," I said, with a grin I couldn't rid myself of while wiping his sperm off my palm on the wall behind me. I thought he was a virgin as I was, but I later found out he meant it was the first time someone wanked him on the street.

We parted ways at the station. I spent the journey home analyzing what had happened that night.

I arrived home and found Suzanna watching a movie in the living room. She laughed upon seeing me so drunk and asked me where I spent my evening and with whom. I grinned back at her and told her I went out with my colleagues and things went wild after few drinks and that all I wanted at that moment was some water and to sleep. So I washed my hands in the kitchen sink after realizing I was still sticky from Richard's cum and headed to bed, where I fell asleep in no time.

I spent that weekend in a vegetative state, trying to recover from a massive hangover. My conversations with Richard slowly died during that weekend, which was somehow convenient for me as I didn't want to meet him again. It was fun. He was great, from what I gathered, but I was not ready to have a relationship while living in a lie regarding my sexuality.

Eight

The first week of April brought with it sunny days and good energy. Suzanna and Thom started going out more often. He got a great manager position in a coffee shop in The City, which allowed them to afford more trips around the UK. That meant more weekends by myself, at home. I liked being alone as I could not feel judge if I wasn't in the mood of doing anything or just wanted to use my dildo – which I named *SinDick*.

Things became complex and challenging at work - while my payment remained unchanged - but I had my friends, Lala and Jakub, who were great fun and supportive. We kept on stopping for a pint on our way home from work, and most of the time, we ended up drunk. I knew I could confide in them regarding my sexuality, but God, it was hard to come to terms with who I was. It's such long progress of analyzing and weighing all possibilities and potential losses you might suffer the moment you go out of your shell, and it can make a man go mad.

On that faithful first Saturday of April, I woke up and found my flatmates preparing breakfast for us. We were to be accompanied by Thom's brother Adrian and their cousin George. I'm not a morning person, and I genuinely need to have at least one hour to put my brain into motion every morning, which meant that I had to rush, have a coffee and a smoke, and jump in the shower to speed up my return to reality.

We broke fast and chatted about how we had all been lately – of course, I lied my ass off and told everyone how great my life was – and heard their plans that reassured me I was to be home alone the entire weekend.

That week, Suzanna asked if I was interested in spending the weekend in Brighton with her sister and the whole gang, but I was short of money and really wanted to stay home and have some time alone. Another invitation was extended by Gorge, considering he was the only one who didn't have a date and felt like a third wheel, but I declined one more time, promising to attend their next escapade.

They left shortly after eleven, and I proceeded with my weekend home alone routine. I went and shaved my ass and balls, trimmed my pubes, and deep-cleaned my pussy.

I was sitting on the roof terrace getting ready for action – looking for porn, smoking, and drinking coffee – when a message notification popped on my phone screen. It was my daddy-neighbor. I thought he vanished in thin air as I haven't seen him online since New Year's Eve.

Him: *Hey, neighbor! How you've been? Glad to find you here. I apologize for disappearing as I did and… for so long. You are cutter than I expected you to be, by the way.*

He made me smile and blush.

Me: *Hello, neighbor! Thanks! I'm good. What about you?*

Him: *I had some family stuff to deal with, but all OK now. Are you discreet? Can you keep a secret?*

Me: *If it's not for me to tell, why would I divulge anyone's secret?*

Him: *Haha! Great answer! I just thought it is only fair to show you this, so you know whom you're talking to.*

So he sent a shirtless photo of him lying in bed, his not too hairy chest popping out, smiling through a short thick beard. His eyes were dark brown, and his hair was cut short. He was one beautiful man. I couldn't believe he considered me cute and that he was still talking to me and entrusting me with his identity.

Me: *Hello there! You look great. Love your eyes…*

Him: *Thanks, but stop. Please don't make me blush! I'm Matt. What's your name?*

Me: *I'm Thom. Nice to meet you.*

Matt: *It would be nicer actually to meet, don't you think?*

Me: *That'll be great, but what about your wife?*

Matt: *No worries. She's out of town for the weekend, and she took the kids with her. So, do you want to meet? Let's say in thirty minutes in front of the petrol station on Lower Richmond Road?*

Me: *See you then! I'll jump in the shower now.*

Matt: *See you soon, gorgeous man.*

I could not believe what had happened. I was to go for a drink with my sexy neighbor, and we were both home alone. Scenarios were taking shape inside my head, and I tried to plan every step of our date: questions, answers, my place or his. I needed to calm myself and just go with the flow. But how could I do that when the excitement was more significant than my self-control?

I rinsed myself and put a clean shirt on, a pair of jeans, and my boots. It was warm outside, but I took my jacket to hide my ever-growing sweat stains under my armpits and left the house.

Walking down the footpath connecting Felsham Road with Upper Richmond Road, I felt my knees weakening. My heart was beating fast. Then, turning left at the end of the street toward the petrol station, I heard a deep man's voice calling my name. Turning around, there he was, walking toward me. Matt looked better in the flesh than in pictures. I felt a rush of heat inundating my face while my heart was on the verge of breaking out my chest and run.

I extended my hand to greet him, and he responded appropriately, then pulled me into an embrace, and kissed my cheek.

"I'm so pleased to meet you," said Matt, with a smile.

He wore a close-fitting T-shirt that accentuated his muscular arms – I have a thing for arms and hands. His subtle perfume inundated my nostrils, making me close my eyes for a second to register it.

"You too," I said in a low voice, overwhelmed by emotions. "Where shall we go?"

"I thought we could grab some beers from the off-license and head to mine so we can sit in the garden away from people's eyes. I promise to behave," he laughed an intoxicating laugh.

"That sounds good," I replied, thinking of how fast my plans and scenarios shuttered.

We went into the shop and grabbed few beers, for which he insisted to pay under the pretext of being the host, and made our way to his place. He lived on Lower Richmond Road, not far from the shop.

We entered his garden via the side gate of the garden. Matt told me to make myself comfortable while he grabbed some glasses, so I took off my jacket that did nothing but accelerated my sweating and sat down at the wooden table in the shade of a big old tree. My legs were shaking; my mouth was dry. I prayed for him not to be disappointed by my looks, and I also prayed for an answer to one fundamental question: what the hell was I doing in this married man's garden?

Matt arrived shortly after, carrying two glasses and a bucket of ice in which he placed the beers to keep the cold. He poured the drinks while enquiring about my age, nationality, hobbies, and career. This made me relax and become more confident. From the moment he came out of the house, he never took his eyes off me. He pulled a chair from underneath the table and placed it before me, leaving a small blank space between us.

Matt was a funny guy. We laughed and talked about various nonsense that makes us who we are. We were three beers down when he laid back in his chair, stretched, and pushed his pelvis upwards, exposing a big bulge. I froze, mesmerized. He came back into his seat and asked me:

"Dou you like what you see?"

The words stumbled on my tongue, and I could not form a sentence. I shook my head in approval.

"Hey, don't be shy now. I like what I see too. I like you," said Matt, placing his palms on my knees squeezing them hard. "I'm going to kiss you now."

We both leaned towards each other, meeting in the middle. Grabbing the back of my head in a firm grasp, he pushed his tongue in my mouth, and slowly, but forcefully he swirled it inside my oral cavity. His kiss excited me, and placing my palms on his hard chest, I let out a moan which signaled my enjoyment and made him press himself harder on my lips. With the other hand, Matt grabbed my already hardened cock and caressed it through my trousers.

He stopped kissing me and looked me in the eyes, smiling.

"Let's see what you can do, my beautiful Romanian boy!" said he, standing up and placing himself closely in front of me, unbuttoning his trousers. I could feel my penis pushing painfully against my tight underwear, trying to break free while my pussy-hole itched with anticipation. The lack of experience intensified my awareness, and my people-pleasing personality surfaced like a coping mechanism.

The man had a big one. There, right in front of my eyes. Matt's cock jumped out of his underpants. Standing to attention was this magnificent shlong of a man that wanted me. I had to do a good job. Placing my hand around his shaft,

I looked up at him with a smile of anticipation – it was thick. Then, with a nod of the head, he gestured me to go for it.

Placing my lips around the tip of his dick, I forced my tongue between the foreskin and the helmet-shaped knob, slowly swirling it in a circular motion while my mouth filled with saliva. He moaned in elation. He took hold of my head with both hands and pushed his cock inside my mouth, commanding me to open it up and take it. He went deep, making me gag and pull back. Tears gathered in my eyes while I gasped for air. Matt laughed contentedly, slapped my face with his phallus, then pushed himself back in my mouth and forcefully fucked it. I kept my breath and forced my jaws wide open to welcome him.

He pulled out and, grabbing me by the chin, brought me up to my feet and said:

"Let's do this inside. The neighbors might hear us."

Matt took my hand and guided me through the house, all the way up to his bedroom. Once there, he asked me to undress in front of him, and I did. I was shy to show my naked body, but the gorgeous daddy bit his lips with desire and pushed me onto the bed upon seeing me. When he placed his hot body on top of me, I opened my legs and wrapped them around his waist, letting our cocks meet. Then, putting two fingers in my mouth, he invited me to suck, then pushed them deeper down my throat and said:

"By the time I finish with you, you'll have no gag reflex."

Standing up by the side of the bed, he grabbed my arms and pulled me on the width of the bed, my head hanging off its side. He commanded me to open my mouth wide and cover my teeth with my lips and place his manhood inside it, pushing it deep with the weight of his body. It felt good; my throat was more relaxed in that position. The straight alignment of my mouth and pharynx facilitated a more manageable, deeper penetration, allowing the entire length of his shaft inside. His cleaned shaved balls were slapping my face while he thrust and thrust, making my eyes water.

When he pulled out, I gulped for air, my face purple, covered in slobber and tears. He wiped it with his hands and turned me around, pushing my feet up, exposing my hole. Matt kneeled on the floor and, placing his face between my butt cheeks, started teasing my sphincter. His short, dense beard increased the pleasure exponentially and the tip of his tongue making its way inside of me made me quiver in anticipation.

When he was done with rimming me, he flipped me around, so I was on my all fours and pressed the small of my back to make me arch it and spat on my pussy. Then, he played with his hardened cock around my whole, making me beg him to penetrate me. Matt laughed and said:

"So impatient!"

In one strong thrust, he impaled me, making sure to hold me in a powerful grasp by my wings so I could move in one direction only, towards him. The pain I felt in my sphincter was excruciating, but he held me there with the entire length of his penis inside of me, telling me to wait and relax while he slowly moved in and out my cunt. I loved the feel of him inside of me, pressing hard on my prostate. I moaned loudly, and so I bit the sheet to stop me from screaming and gave in. He fucked me better than I managed to do it myself with my dildo when the realization hit me: it was a hundred times better to be fucked by the real thing rather than a silicone one.

The euphoric state I found myself in made me forget about protection, and it was too late. He came inside of me, his hot cum filling up my cavity like expanding foam. When he pulled out, he told me to clench and keep his seed inside of me. He collapsed on the bed and hugged me from behind. He kissed me on the neck and asked if I was alright. Well, I was more than that. I was rhapsodically satisfied.

"I want you to keep that fathering load inside of you all day so you can feel me there with every step you take," Matt said while I stood there in his solid and rugged arms studying the wedding band on his finger, "and take a video of it coming out your pussy when it does and send it to me."

"Yes… daddy," I said, giggling, which made him laugh.

He produced a pack of wet wipes from the nightstand, took one, and offered me the rest so I can clean my ass while he cleaned his cock. Then, we dressed, and he accompanied me to the garden gate where he kissed me goodbye and thanked me for coming over. Before I left, Matt asked me for my phone number and gave me his so I could send him the video he requested and promised to contact me next time his wife was away.

I went home and jumped in the shower. The hot water falling down my head and sticky body made me unwind, and I felt my sore vaginanus opening slightly. I squeezed it and clenched my butt cheeks to avoid spilling Matt's seed. My cock hardened in a second, so I closed my eyes and masturbated, thinking of the married man and his wood inside me, of his touch and dominating nature.

Later that afternoon, after waking up from a much-needed nap, I took my phone and, squatting on top of it, I recorded the cum squirting out of me.

I sent the video to Matt with the caption: *You were fantastic. Thanks again.* He didn't reply straight away as I expected him to do. I started asking myself why and tried to come up with an array of excuses for him but realized that I could not let this affect me in any way. It was just a hook-up with a married man, and I should forget about it. No way he would ever contact me again, and there was no future for us no matter how much I liked him and enjoyed being with him that day.

Matt went silent, and I carried on with my weekend, beating myself down once more with my looks, sexuality, and life I lead.

Nine

The more time I spent on dating apps, the more insecure and unworthy I felt. After meeting Matt, I could not get him out of my head and tried my luck to contact him again a week later, but in vain, so I turned my attention to the internet. I searched and tried to meet other men, but all my efforts lead nowhere.

The discouragement was overwhelming, and from what I gathered from men's profiles, the chances to find someone to like me for who I was were slim. Men that attracted me were not interested and ignored me or cut short our conversations. I thought I had a problem, that I had to change, be more likable and malleable, and shapeshift according to others' interests.

When you are chubby and have been that way all your life, it is hard to change your habits and start exercising. So the only thing I could do was to starve myself to lose some weight.

The alcohol was not an addiction – or at least I did not see it as one at that point – so I continued drinking the way I did, a couple of glasses of wine a day or few small beers to keep me going and happy. My smoking… yes, it was a massive part of who I was. A disgusting habit that affects your life in many ways, but being a self-destructive person, I could not push myself to quit, seeing smoking as the only freedom I had left.

At night, when I sat in bed trying to fall asleep, my mind started working, and I often analyzed myself, my past and present, my failed and unaccomplished dreams, and how unfair everything was for me.

It might sound tedious or not, but I didn't know what was wrong with me. I know I might need professional help or advice, but the pressure I have put on me throughout the years has turned the happy child I once knew into a defective adult. I had people in my life telling me how great I am as a person, how beautiful I am, and how good I am at my job, professional, determined, and hard-working. But, unfortunately, I never believed them and still cannot take a compliment. I just fuss and turn away when someone says a good thing about me in my presence.

Nowadays, we tend to create something new on a saturated market, reinvent the classics, who we are, and how people should live their lives. We deconstruct dishes, set stronger boundaries around the definition of normality, and push the odd ones out of society by bullying them, making them feel worthless. I know my background and how strange it was for me to come to puberty and realize that I was different, not normal.

I keep sometimes wondering if, in this deconstructed world divided by hate and greed, by financial status, religion, skin color, sexual orientation, and many more, there is a slight chance for someone like me to find a way of living, of picking up the pieces and reconstruct myself in a way I could fit in the bigger picture, blend in the world and be accepted.

In Romania, like everywhere else at one point, it used to be illegal to be gay, and that happened not long ago, and, plus in other countries, it still is. I grew up in a middle-class family on the outskirts of a small town in Transylvania. My mother always wanted a daughter and prayed for it while pregnant with me – maybe that's why we are born gay. A divine entity punishes our mothers for their sins by messing up their embryos, creating us. I turned out to be a boy, and from a young age, I liked having my nails painted, playing with my mother's shoes and clothes, dolls over football. For my family, it wasn't something weird at all. I was a kid, and kids play with what they have and want, so they let me be. Every time I went out with my parents, meeting acquaintances along the way, I was told with admiration that I was pretty like a girl and looked exactly like my mother. I have to agree with them partially. I'm like my mother: we both like cock.

I wish things were easier for us, the outcasts, but as the old saying goes, *what doesn't kill you, makes you stronger.* Who I am, the choices I made, the people and places, the secrets I kept, the masks I wear, the bridges I built or burnt made me and built my personality and did not kill me yet. Yet! I thought of ending it, putting a stop to the struggle, and believe me when I say that it wasn't easy to step back. I believe what kept me from doing it is my unselfishness and the fear of hurting those that care about me. Of course, I would not like to see my best friends and family crying after me, but this thought is getting thinner when throwing in the mix of adulthood, responsibilities, and the tall walls I erected to keep myself hidden.

I am grateful to those who fought and died for us to have it easier today as gays, have rights, and be accepted, and the regret is that I could not be home and have what I have in London. I had to turn my life upside-down and start from scratch, and I sensed I was making the same mistakes over and over again. I mainly spent my formative years being different and headed into my teens emotionally crippled, and now it was the time for me to reboot.

Matt was the man that started it all. Looking at his wedding band resting on his finger, strangling it, I wondered how life must be for him, what does he feel, does his wife know and accepts it, does he do what he did with me on a regular basis, and was I just another guy he fucked? What about his kids? I sunk in thoughts and meditated over his life as it would be mine and could not conceive the perfect picture of a happy ending.

The online dating sucked, and I was not made for it, but what other chances one has to meet someone in a bar or club in these modern times? I know of their existence but never went in one. I knew I would not fit in there whatsoever. Looking in the mirror, I always saw a defective appearance and an unlovable person. If I don't love myself, how could someone do it?

Maybe Carmen was right when she said that *a man like you will die alone.*

Towards the end of April, I resumed my online search, but this time I wanted more substance from a date, not just hook-ups. My tactic was simple: to be honest about whom I was, with good and bad, and connect and chat with those that picked my interest, and if after a short conversation I felt it might go somewhere, I would ask to meet for a drink. Taking the date from online to offline makes a difference. It is much more revealing when you see a person face to face. It saves time and energy for both of you. One thing I had to keep in mind: not to have any expectations. That was hard, but I had to try and do it. Online people tend to lie; it is easy to do so and even easier to portray a person you know your correspondent might like so you can get them into your bed.

By the beginning of May, I had two dates with some cute Latino men. They were exciting and funny, but the downside of it all was we were all bottoms. After feeling a strong connection with someone, that moment of realization is so uncomfortable when you understand you are not sexually compatible. So we parted ways laughing and wishing each other the best of luck in finding the tops that would have us.

I was on my way home from the date with the second cutie when I received a text from Matt: *Hey. Hope you are well. Just wanted to let you know I tested positive for Chlamydia. You should get tested too. Don't text back. My wife is around. Good luck!*

The sky fell on my head. I heard of chlamydia before but had no clue about the severity of it and treatment. Plus, I had no knowledge of the medical system in the UK; I wasn't even registered with a GP (general practitioner). Panicked, I sat down on a bench and lit a cigarette, took my phone out of my pocket, and searched the symptoms, effects, and course of treatment for this nightmare. As a word of advice: never check with Doctor Google your symptoms or any diseases. Better dig your own grave as that is more reassuring. It was unbearable and felt heavy on my chest to know I had no close friend to ask for advice, guidance, or help without being asked the circumstances I might have got the STI, so I decided to text my date and ask him. I felt shame and terror by doing so and wanted to bury my head in the sand and stay there.

Amused by my words, he called me and, choking on his laughter, asked me what happened. I told him about the text and how I knew nothing of what I could do. He then explained how I should not stress about it and just go to a free clinic on Dean Street, down in Soho. We finished the conversation with him telling me that this was the best end of a date he ever had and for what it was worth, he was happy to have helped me with it.

The next day I presented myself at the clinic. I was nervous. The chances of someone recognizing me were slim to none, but I am paranoid and had no chance but stressed about it.

At the reception, a young lady with a white lab coat casually resting on her shoulders, allowing her black see-through top to stand out, welcomed me with a smile. She asked me about myself and my concerns. I told her I was new in the country and that it was my first time in a clinic. She then produced a "loyalty card" – as I liked to call it – took my details and asked me why I went there that day. Finally, in a slow whisper, I admitted to having intercourse with someone that tested positive for chlamydia and was guided downstairs to the waiting room where I was to wait for someone to call my name.

The nervous state intensified with each step I took but finally landed in the basement of the clinic where a bunch of men, all with their faces buried in their phones, were waiting patiently and in complete silence. When I arrived, they all glanced at me and checked me out while I turned lobster red and looked for a corner to hide from their prying eyes. Forty minutes later, a nurse called my name and directed me to a consultation room. I walked fast, almost ran through the mass of men.

The nurse was kind, which made the experience much more bearable. I told her my story, she took my details and informed me about the treatment. I got offered the option to have an HIV test, which I accepted out of politeness. Due to my self-destructive nature, I knew I would have lived happily, not knowing if I was positive or not. A positive test would have killed me before the disease got a chance. She handed me the medication for a two-week antibiotic treatment and a test and told me to go upstairs to the toilets and do the swab off all my cavities.

Thanks to the video guide in the toilet, I managed to swab my mouth, penis, and ass – not with the same swab, thankfully – and left the test next to the reception to be taken for analysis. Then, I walked out through the entrance doors wishing the receptionist a beautiful weekend. As I stepped on the pavement, I walked as fast as possible to distance myself from the place. I didn't want to be seen walking out of the clinic.

The results for both tests came in the next day. They were negative but still had to follow the treatment for two weeks as prevention. I told myself at the moment that from then on, my slutty butt will only take in a cock that is neatly tucked in a condom, to avoid putting myself through that again – which I did, but that's another story.

Ten

As the days rolled into May, I found it hard to bear the slow passing of time. Growing up in Romania in a small town with no cinema, one swimming pool, and too many banks and corner shops for the number of citizens, I never learned to keep myself busy and help the time pass faster by being productive. I liked watching TV and run through the forest with my friends, but my main activity was dreaming. I dreamt of growing up, of being a girl (which would have made my life much more accessible and tolerable), meeting the love of my life, starting a family, and having a successful career as a celebrity chef. My friend Lala now calls me 'Celebrity Chef Thomas' after succeeding in becoming a recognized asset to the business I worked for, and maybe she was doing it out of jealousy even though she never struck me at being the kind.

I had huge dreams, which were supported by a mediocre ambition to succeed. I remember being around twelve when I first started turning my big goose-feather stuffed pillow into a boyfriend – called Nick. I went to bed every night and hugged it, creating a fantasy where we were free to love each other in a world of acceptance and accomplishment. I look back to that time and wonder if it is a dream still worth fighting for, considering its influence on my decision to move to London.

Things were good at work, and after months of hard work and dedication (I had nothing else better to do with my time but throw myself headfirst in every aspect of the catering business while caring for my duties as a pastry chef), my efforts were recognized. An article about me appeared on the company's blog, making my parents, friends, and former teachers proud. My bond with Lala and Jakub grew stronger with each weak spent together, and I thought I could trust them with my secret but still had to wait for the right time to tell them. I wasn't ready yet.

My time off was filled with the endless search of Mr. Right and concocting new lies to cover my true identity and activities from the increasingly nosy flatmates. Somehow I managed to get away with weeknight dates under the pretext of having drinks with my colleagues after work. My weekend activities were easier to hide from them thanks to their eventful life, always being interested in meeting people, visiting places, and partying – I went with them a few times, but frankly, I had much more pressing desires and dreams and being in their company for extended periods of time was pushing me to detest my life more and more, feeling I could never achieve their level of happiness as a couple. We connected and established a good friendship but always felt inferior to them and a liar. Still, my ever-growing fear of being utterly alone in the world, as I felt sometimes, turned me into a pleaser and a good companion for others. This resulted in me being overly generous with others and consistently placing myself and my needs on the second plan, chipped away at my self-esteem and self-worth in vast amounts. I wish I had someone to confide in and tell me when to stop, every time I went overboard with my self-imposed altruism.

The time spent on the hook-up app became dull. I saw the same profiles from around my neighborhood, many of them belonging to men out of my league. So I turned my attention to other dating apps, where I successfully matched and conversed with some attractive men from further afield.

On a Saturday afternoon, right after Suzanna and Thom left in one of their weekend trips, I received a message from a twenty-four-year-old top (after his description). I was aware of his existence as he had texted me before trying to hook up by sending me his location and a few pictures with him in a leather harness, which I ignored. However, this time he took a different approach. He started a conversation more to my liking: inquiring about my day, hobbies, and other generalities, expanding into a more philosophical one about life, wellbeing, and the Universe, jumping to sexual preferences when the conversation stalled.

Without telling him about our earlier virtual encounter, I took the chance to say to him that I rather meet him for a drink than spend time chatting away online. He agreed, and we met that afternoon in a pub located midway between our houses. I wanted to meet him to satisfy my curiosity about men like him, those that go all in for a quickie by sending their location to strangers.

As the sun started setting and the sky turned ruby red, I walked towards Putney Common and met Liam. He was taller than me, skinny but fit with a shaved head and dark eyes. We shook hands upon meeting, and after the brief greetings, I could not but notice that his voice was high-pitched for my liking, plus a bit camp. I thought at the time that this could be a NO when it came to the man I wanted, but considering my strict agenda and not wishing to move forward after this date, I came to ignore this about him.

We grabbed a beer at the counter and sat outside on the benches set on the little field across from the pub. He was very charming, confident, and shown an interest in me which took me by surprise. I talked about myself for an extended period, and seeing that he was a primary school teacher, Liam never hesitated to correct my English under the pretext of helping me improve my speech. I welcomed with shame his input and went with the flow.

What was supposed to be a short date with a strict plan on my behalf turned into a full-on one with debates, stories of the past, laughter, and booze. As the alcohol clouded my brain, I let go of inhibitions, feeling free and gay in front of the young man who sat in front of me. With the setting of the sun, an urge for sexual contact with him took over my body, but I knew I had to control it and tried to put an end to the date. Finally, he agreed to leave only with the condition of meeting again on Sunday for another date.

Arriving home, all I could think about was him and how much I liked him. It felt true for the first time that the good will come your way the moment you stop searching for it. So I went to bed with his image in my head and started touching myself, wanking while thinking of him.

The following day at noon, Liam picked me up with his small Woltz Vagen and promised to take me to a place I never went before. Under the last night's agreement of just dating to get to know each other better before advancing to the next steps of a relationship, I knew he wouldn't try to take me to a place and fuck me, even if I was prepared for such an occasion. Blame me or not, but in my opinion, being a good bottom is always to be ready for penetrative sex no matter the circumstances. Unfortunately, I don't have the advantage of a vagina, almost always ready for a cock so, I treated my ass as one making do with what I had.

As we drove towards our destination, I tried and begged him to tell me where he was taking me but with no success.

"A surprise qualifies as one until revealed, so do not expect me to ruin it for you. Have patience, and let me do something nice for you," Liam said, smiling, trying to stop me from pushing him to reveal his intent.

"Can we listen to some music so I can stop thinking of where you're taking me?"

"Yaaas! I have my favorite music right here," he said enthusiastically.

The music he played was nothing of my liking. I'm an 80's music lover with few modern artists like Adele, Birdy, Pink, Lady Gaga, and Florence and the Machine picking my interest and touching the right spots of my soul, while Liam was obsessed with contemporary music, especially with Little Mix. People judged me for it, but I'm not too fond of their music, and I can't explain why. I just don't like it, and that is it.

I suffered in silence while my ears bled and Liam danced and sang, wishing for an ice-pick bursting my eardrums and pricing deep inside my brain to be the surprise.

We arrived at Richmond Park a few minutes later. He had chosen to take me there and be the first that shows me around after learning the previous day that I never visited it, even if the park was so close to my home. We parked the car and went for a walk. The weather was on our side, and the May sun brought nature back to life after the long-dormant state in winter. The air was fresh and clean, making me lightheaded. We strolled down the paths and talked about music when I confessed my dislikes. He tried to show understanding but slightly criticized my tastes, telling me I wasn't a sixty years old gay man and I should grow up.

Our travels and conversations made us thirsty, and upon arriving closer to the center of the park, we spotted an ice-cream van and stopped for a whippy. Sat down underneath a tree, we ate the sweet, cold treats and watched the deer grazing silently in the distance. Liam shifted the conversation from music to friends and how he liked to spend his time off, telling me that he would have plenty of time to party and had even planned a week holiday in Ibiza with the upcoming summer school holiday. He was the type of person with commitment issues, appreciating his freedom and wanting to hold on to it at any cost. I didn't grasp that at the time. Instead, I was charmed by him and his wittiness and dreamt of having him as a lover - a confident man by my side to lean on and build a forever-lasting relationship with.

Exhausted by thirst and walk and considering he was living at the edge of the park, Liam invited me to his flat for a drink with the promise of driving me home afterward.

A six-story building triumphed over the landscape as we turned the corner and drove towards a private parking area. We entered through the main entrance silently, with him leading the way. My thoughts were mixed but what popped out from the amalgam was that we never kissed, which couldn't lead to more than that. So I instated on the spot the third date rule – no sex until then. As the elevator doors opened, Liam placed a hand on my lower back and gently pushed me inside. He stepped in, pressed the button for the sixth floor, and turned to face me. Pinning me to the mirrored wall, Liam kissed me hungrily, pushing his tongue deep inside my mouth. The elevator dinged as we reached our destination, and he broke off the kiss by spinning around on his heels and went out.

The flat was nice and clean and smelled fresh. I read the signs in the smell of homes: a fresh smelling one is a sign of happiness and good company; a food smell is a sign of 'still living with my mother'; while a stinky place is a sign of depression and poor hygiene and I should run for my life.

Liam directed me through the living room to the balcony and went to bring some beers from the kitchen. I examined the simplicity of the room's design, feeling the place's coldness through the lack of personal items in the shared space. You could easily see that few individuals rented the flat, and no one tried to make it feel like home. Besides two sofas with a glass coffee table in the middle, a dining table pushed in a corner at the back of the room, and one massive flat screens TV, there were no personal items to spruce up the room or reveal the identity of the household.

We sat and enjoyed a cold drink and a smoke on the two rickety chairs on the balcony while Liam went on talking, sharing one too many details of his friends and the good times he has when going out with them. Little did I know that he was paving the way to his freedom while keeping me of use at the same time. We retreated in the comfort of his house and snuggled on the sofa. He took hold of me, and climbing slowly on top of me, kissed me passionately. I felt my hot blood pumping in my ears and groin making my cock harden while pre-cum stained my underwear. With a swift move of hands, Liam undid my pants and, pushing his hand underneath me, made his way to my butthole, starting massaging it intensely. I moaned in desire and kissed him harder and harder with each pressing of my sphincter. Finally, he pulled his hand out from underneath me, stood up, and grabbing my hands, pulled me to my feet and said:

"I think we should take this to the bed."

Holding my trousers with one hand while holding him with the other, we walked out of the living room, and after crossing the hallway, we entered his room. The small place was surgically clean; the furniture was minimal: a double bed, a desk, and a built-in closet with high mirror doors. He closed the door behind us and twisted the key. I was standing in front of him, fluttering nervously from one foot to the other, still holding my unbuttoned jeans. I felt a change in him, one that I liked: he became dominant, sure on himself, in control, and I thought that all I could do was obey him.

"Take off your clothes and let me see you," Liam said in a low-pitched voice, utterly different than the voice I heard before. I feared for a split second that he was possessed.

I complied and took off my trousers and undies, trying to leave my T-shirt on (feeling fatter than ever in his presence), but he ordered me to take it off. Standing there in front of me was a different man than the one I kissed earlier on the couch. He took off his clothes while I watched him. His body showed no traces of fat, just prominent lean muscles. His chest was hairy, his pubes trimmed short, his erected manhood was long and thin. I felt ashamed for staring at him, admiring his body, so I shifted my gaze to the floor. He approached me dauntlessly and pulled me towards him, our bodies touching. Liam kissed me feverously.

I broke off his embrace right on time for him to place his strong hands on my shoulders, and, pressing me to my knees, he took hold of his imposing penis and started slapping me on my mouth with it.

"Open it!" he said while hitting me harder with his wood. "Open it and suck it!"

I did as told and stretched my mouth to welcome his long cock. As I reached to grasp it with one hand, he said:

"No hands. I want you to take it all."

"I don't think I cou…"

Liam stopped me from speaking by pushing his manhood inside my mouth. He did it with such force that it went all in and choked me.

'Choke on it but don't vomit on my dick, cunt!' Liam said and slapped me on the face while I sucked him.

Yanking me to my feet, he pushed me on the bed and kneeled next to it. He then took my cock in his mouth and sucked on it aggressively, stoking it simultaneously. I never experienced a blowjob before, and the excitation and feel of his tongue on my knob made my hair stand on end while I clenched my fists and stiffened my body, curving my spine. Finally, he stopped at my swift movements and, grabbing my thighs, lifted my legs and told me to hold them to my chest while he buried his face between my buttocks, feasting on my posthole.

When he finished licking it, he spat on it and gently inserted his middle finger inside it, slowly rotating it to make sure I get loose enough to welcome him inside. He then forced in a second, followed by a third finger making me moan louder and louder.

'Are you ready to be fucked?' he asked me in the same new voice. 'Do you want me to rip your pussy, boy?'

'Yes, please...' I said quietly.

He took out a small black traveling purse from the desk drawer unit from which he produced some condoms and a small, brown glass bottle with a black and red label. He ripped off the condom's pack with his teeth, placed it on his cock, opened the suspicious bottle, and placed it on one nostril. He sniffed, repeating the process with the other nostril. He then shoved the bottle in my snout and said:

'Sniff it! It will help you relax and take it.'

'I don't do drugs,' I said defensively, but he covered my mouth with the other hand and waited for me to break and breathe in. Unfortunately, the vapors irritated my nose and made me cough. Almost instantly, the substance made me drowsy. I blamed it on him for making me inhale it in significant amounts, but I was too aroused to care by the end of it and waited for him to set the poppers on the table and penetrate me.

Liam pushed his fully erect penis in me without taking the time to think of my need to get used to it, to enjoy a slow penetration, and get accustomed to his size. I screamed in pain and tried to pull back from his grasp but couldn't. Besides his looks, Liam was stronger than I anticipated. To prove his dominance, he thrust deep inside me, transforming my pain into pleasure. He went deep, and his hardwood, though thinner than I liked one to be, massaged my prostate, making me want more and more. Then, with a sudden move, he grabbed me by my ass while my feet rested on his shoulders and lifted me from the bed, letting the weight of my body (and I'm not a skinny guy) fall down on his manhood and penetrated me broadly. My heart skipped a beat, thinking I was about to break him and his wand, but that wasn't the case. He wanted me there, wanted to prove to me who's in charge and how good a fucker he was.

Putting me back on the bed, he placed a pillow underneath the small of my back and, kneeling between my legs, shoved himself inside me once more. Then, with fast movements, he started fucking me as no one did before. I screamed and moaned in ecstasy, feeling my ass burn but didn't want him to stop. Liam asked:

"Can I cum inside? I need to cum…" he said through gapping breaths. "Can I?"

"Yes! Please… Yes!" I moaned.

Pulling himself out of me, he took off the condom and penetrated me again, thrusting harder and harder. I felt his hot semen deep in my rectum, my pussy all wet and aching.

Letting out a conquering growl, Liam smiled and collapsed on my chest, saying:

"You really are something. I'm glad you let go of your prejudices and opened up for me. Did you like it?"

I couldn't but smile and nod my head in approval. I pulled back, allowing his cock to tumble out of me. We fell asleep like that, glued together by our sweat and bodily fluids. When I woke up, he was in the shower, so I took my clothes from the floor and dressed up, getting ready to leave the flat and head home. I started thinking of a lie to tell at home if my flatmates were there upon my arrival.

That evening, sat on the terrace smoking, I thought of him, of us, the sex and the fun we had together, falling in the love trap I wanted to. Liam dominated my thoughts from then on, and I tried to be cool with it, not showing him how much he obsessed me. We started a relationship in which I wanted him for more than sex. I can't say the same for him.

Liam was that guy that plays hard to get. I texted him every day and night, trying to make him meet me, but he never had time whenever I asked him. We only met when he wanted, and I obliged him. The sex continued to be intense even though it felt as I was sleeping with someone else due to his transformation during intercourse. The man I went for walks and dinners with vanished every time we were naked, being replaced by that second personality, an obsessed, commanding, and controlling top male.

The end of June came upon us with great excitement from his side while I dreaded the moment. His Ibiza holiday approached faster than ever. Liam never asked me to go with him. I knew how important his friends are to him, but I always thought that one would know their partner's pals in a relationship. Unfortunately, this was not the case here. In six, seven weeks of pretending we were a thing, Liam never asked me out to meet his companions. Those people always came before me, my needs and desires. I understood him just because I kept him a secret from everyone.

The night before his departure, I offered to make some pizza at his place and maybe watch a movie with his flatmates. That evening was a mess, and I made a fool of myself. After buying all the necessary ingredients to make pizza from scratch, I went to him and threw myself in the kitchen while he and the gang were watching TV in the living room. I am not a friendly person, quite an introvert at heart, so being left alone was my choice. It took me more than two hours to make the food. I had no baking paper to line the trays, and I had to improvise a rolling pin to do my job.

When the pizza was ready and the boys chose the movie we were to watch, I asked Liam to help me cut and plate the food in the kitchen. I felt so ashamed and stupid when the makeshift baking paper stuck to the dough, and I needed to flip the pizza, toping down, to be able to peel it off. The food looked like a rhinoceros sat on it, but we were hungry and ate it anyway.

Liam and his flatmates, Lucas and David, made fun of me and my cooking skills and asked how I became a pastry chef. It was hurtful, but I took it with a smile. I left their flat before midnight, wishing them all a great time in Ibiza, and headed home praying to God to wash away this night from everyone's memory.

I think my prayers were misunderstood and had a much undesired strong effect upon them all. In ten days spent alone thinking of and texting him, Liam called me once, very briefly, and texted twice. I did not know what to make of his behavior, and knowing how raw our relationship was, I started thinking of him cheating on me. I spent my days and nights imagining him fucking strangers in the hotel room, taking part in orgies, and feeding his cum to hungry sluts. The anger and frustration grew inside me despite my constant forced reassurance that he would not do such things.

It took me more than a week to see him after his holiday was over. We met on the riverside in Barnes, me delighted to see him; he was ignorant of my feelings. Liam couldn't stop talking about how fun it was to be free and told me all about their time in Ibiza, how cool his friends are, and all the jokes that made him piss himself laughing. I stood there in front of this man that stole my heart, crying inside, fearing the fast-approaching end of our relationship.

Eleven

Feeling his lies intensifying and realizing his avoidance of seeing me outside his room, I grew jealous and frustrated. Was there something wrong with me that made this man not wanting me? Was I just another foreigner in his world as I was in his country? Was I not good enough and worthy of his love?

I knew I had my issues about my sexuality, but I simply dreamt of being caught kissing a man rather than coming out to my friends in an awkward conversation. It was just easier for me to get over the giant wall I've put between me and those I cared about, and Liam turned out not to be the one I would kiss in front of them.

One weeknight in mid-July, Liam called me to ask if I would like to go for a walk around my neighborhood. He sounded sad, and I wanted to be there for him. So I threw on some clothes and rushed outside to meet him on Putney Bridge.

He did look upset when I saw him from a distance. His shoulders and head were pushed forward, a sign of heavy thoughts pressing on his mind. I approached him like a lion approaches its prey, not wanting to startle him. When I was in his sight, he straightened up and welcomed me with a kiss and an arrogant attitude. Then, asking him what had happened, he started telling me a story of one of his many Berlin trips in which he went to gay parties, completely naked, hanging around with his jewels exposed, and how all the men around him approached him for one thing only: the size of his cock. He felt nothing but used after those experiences, like the world didn't give a shit about who he truly was, and this thought had haunted him ever since, but lately, it got stronger.

Upon hearing this story, I couldn't but wonder what the problem actually was. Or was there a problem? Was he trying to tell me he is not proud of the size of his cock? Or was he telling me this to see how I react? Was Liam missing a loving and caring relationship? That was what I tried offering him, but he stopped all my attempts. Or was another way of telling me that he is too good in bed, that he feels responsible for sharing it with others and not being stuck in a monogamous relationship?

I hugged him and told him how I felt, told him I cared deeply for him, even went as far as implying that I started developing deeper fillings. Of course, I meant love, but somehow all the thoughts spun my head like a washing machine, and I couldn't bring myself in admitting such a thing to him. It was way too early and fresh between us, and in all this time, he didn't treat me quite as I expected to be treated by my partner.

We parted ways after a short walk and headed straight to bed, where I took my thoughts underneath the covers and started processing. The following week, after another period of excuses and statements of how much he needs to go and see his friends rather than seeing me, I grew more and more frustrated. I wanted to check on him and see if he was alright and maybe to have some sex. I longed for his touch, for the Liam behind closed doors but, had no luck. That Saturday, he had to go out clubbing with his friends, some sort of coming-out party for a good friend of his.

After another weird conversation on how he needs his friends more than me, I went mental. I re-downloaded my dating apps (which I deleted in front of him when we decided to dedicate ourselves to each other), with the intent of spying on him. I had an itch that needed scratching. I did not need to wait for long to see his profile active; he was online on the hooking-up app. Fuming, I messaged him, *Hello,* and the reply came in no time: he blocked me. I then texted him on his phone, and he denied it. I could not believe it. What a cunt!

I went back on the app and, under many flushes of rage, I contacted a random guy and checked if he cares for a drink. Yes, I got myself a date for Sunday as he was attending a wedding on Saturday. A revenge date with a stranger was all I needed to hurt Liam as much as he hurt me. I have no idea from where this behavior surfaced. I never saw myself becoming that type of person: a vengeful and mean little prick.

On Sunday at 2 pm, I met Patrick at the Wetherspoons Putney near the bridge. I was ready for sex if the opportunity arose. I made sure to tell Liam I made plans with my friends for that day when he texted me he was hangover and wanted me next to him, to care for him.

Patrick was a nice guy. Same height, tattoos on his arms, a cheeky smile, blue eyes, and a wittiness about himself that soften me. We talked for seven hours about ourselves, his ambitious plans (he was training to go and climb the Everest that August – which was amazing!), my lame plans of becoming a better person. In that time, Liam vanished from my mind but not from my phone, texting me every hour, checking on my wellbeing.

The date went well. We got drunk and started making out on the terrace in front of other customers, without me thinking of hiding. It was past nine when we got kicked out of the pub for being drunk and clumsy, which we found so funny we laughed so much I haven't realized we started walking aimlessly towards Wandsworth. We stopped in darker areas of the street to kiss and hug, we joked about me and my drunkenness, we laughed a bit more. Before I wanted to let him know I would head home, we arrived in front of Wandsworth Park. It was dark outside, and the streets were pretty empty. In a surge of excitement and arousal, he pulled me by the hand, and we went deep inside the park. Reaching a bench, he stopped, turned around, and started kissing me. I felt my cock throbbing in my pants as he began caressing it, and I did the same. Patrick pulled down my trousers, took out my hardening cock, and after lowering himself in front of me, started sucking it.

My heart beat fast as cars drove by in the distance. The adrenaline flood I experienced woke me up from my drunkenness. I pulled him up to his feet and saw his cock already standing on attention, and went down on him. Then, something hard hit my front tooth. I stopped and asked:

"What's that?"

"It's a piercing, don't worry. I have them everywhere," Patrick replied, chuckling.

I struggled to suck him as the metal rod was in the way. When I paused to catch my breath, he pulled me up, turned his back at me, and bent over with his bare ass sticking out like a cat's before mating, indicating me to fuck him. Lubricating his pussy and my penis with saliva, he grasped my wood and directed it to his hole. I pushed slowly and broke in, thrusting in repetitive and calm motion. All I could think of while fucking him was how much I wasn't enjoying it and what I could do to stop. I faked cumming – if there is such a thing – and stood inside waiting for him to do the same. We pulled our pants back on and rushed to the exit. I couldn't believe our luck: as we exited the park, a dog walker entered. Was that good timing, coincidence, or luck… we will never know. As we approached the main street, Patrick invited me to his place to continue our date in a more private setting. I excused myself and told him that I had to wake up early the following day. We said goodbye after exchanging phone numbers and went our separate ways.

On my way home, I took the time to text Liam and told him I was OK, not to be concerned and that I was to go to bed as I was drunk and needed sleep. He replied:

"Good night! I hope you had a great time with your friend. Speak tomorrow. Love you."

Love you?! I couldn't believe my eyes. Did he mean that, or was the text supposed to reach his mother? I was devastated at the sight of his words. How can this be? Did he love me? I knew my fillings for him but was he playing me once more just to get me into his bed?

I went to sleep covered in guilt for what I have done that day. I sought revenge and ended up feeling like shit, full of remorse and dismay.

"This won't be easy to deal with, you fucking slut!" I said to myself the following day. I went to work as it was Monday and was welcomed by Lala, who was concerned by the worrying look on my face. I reassured her it was just a hangover and that I shall recover by tomorrow.

The day went on at a slower than usual pace, and the guilt grew exponentially as the end of the working hours approached. I planned to go home and call Liam to speak with him about his text and see where we were in our relationship. Maybe even confess what a vengeful slut I was.

I'll never forget that afternoon. I arrived at Putney Bridge Station around 4 pm, grabbed a coffee from the bakery across the street from the station, and sat on a bench beside the foot of the bridge. My heart was racing when I picked up the phone and pressed the call button.

Liam failed to answer. I lit a cigarette and sipped my coffee, contemplating my life choices, especially those I made in the last 24 hours, waiting for Liam to return my call. It never happened, but instead, I received a message. With shaking hands and strangled by emotions, I opened the text that read: *Just wanted to tell you something and I hope you'll understand. Last Saturday I did meet up with a guy but it wasn't actually a date… it was a guy I connected with right after our first date. And we have been chatting ever since so I said we could have some dinner and he wanted to take me to see a movie. So I was like sure (he knows I'm dating you).*

My eyes swelled up, and tears rolled down my cheeks. I couldn't believe he had done that, and at the same time, a sense of relief occurred. I started feeling lighter and more relaxed with every tear I shed. The text went on: *You need to understand that I care for you and you have been a summer romance that has meant so much to me and the last thing I have ever wanted to do is hurt you! I'm angry at myself because you are literally the perfect guy and somehow, I just didn't feel the flame. And it makes me incredibly annoying because there are so many fucking twats out there. I want to say this, and then I'll leave you alone. Literally this is no reflection on you. You are sweet and wonderful and kind and caring and everything a man should be but for some bizarre reason, I just didn't see the spark and I was trying to see if it would come. I feel horrendous because you opened up your heart to me. I have been absolutely dedicated to you since day one, and you are amazing in the bedroom (and there's a lot to compare with!), and it upsets me I don't feel more for you. I will leave you alone now and I am truly sorry – the last thing I would ever want to do is upset or hurt you. If you ever want to, I'm here for you as a friend, and I'm a great one of those.*

Oh Lord in Havens and above, what alleviation! I was still crying, but this time the tears turned from bitter to sweet. I felt free of commitment and guilt, knowing he never loved me and that my reckless actions would have never hurt him in any way. I texted him the following: *Thanks for everything babe.*

The time spent together was amazing. I don't hate you. It just wasn't meant to be. Honestly, I'm okay with it. I somehow expected this to happen as I wasn't 100% there anyway, and I always felt a bit pushy towards you as I was trying to make you open up to me. But, you know, I'm a grown-up man, and I can take it. All it's left to do right now is for you to think and focus on yourself, and I'll work on me and my future because time goes on with or without us. Take care of yourself, babe. Bye.

Wiping my face with the back of my hands, I stood up, took a deep breath, and exhaled the frustrations and nervousness that dominated my soul. It was over. He never loved me, and somehow I felt I never truly loved him. It must have been obsession or just despair. I wanted to be loved and to love for so long that I picked the first one that gave me a chance to prove my worth, and I jumped head-first in a shallow river trying to gain the most wanted feeling. I messed up, I know, but I can't force anyone to love me, can I? Maybe if it turns out that I am a psychopath. I will kidnap someone just to make him love me out of fear.

Twelve

With my birthday rapidly approaching, I took a break from online dating and focused on more important things such as my friends and myself. Wanting to lose some weight, I started swimming, as this was the only sport I liked. I felt the need to get in a better mental and physical shape. I planned my birthday with the help of my ever-loving flatmates and tried to push myself out from the gutters I had fallen into.

On the 24th, a handful of friends showed up at my door, dressed in summer clothes, bearing gifts and joy for my special day. It was an intense evening of debate, clatter, and laughter, as many of them met for the very first time. My soul exploded with gratitude for having such amazing people in my life. For the first time, I felt as I achieved something beyond my comprehension: I had a bunch of people I loved and loved me unconditionally, people I could rely on in case the world stopped spinning.

I catered for them all evening and got high on their sweet words and wishes. I wanted to sit them all down and tell them whom they were celebrating, but the fear of losing them then and there stopped me and turned my happiness into sour thoughts of mourning. Would I ever be able to come out and not care about what others think of me?

I cursed my roots and heritage, upbringing, and Christian education that made me hate myself for what I am. If the God I was taught to believe in exists, why does he create gays, bisexuals, and the entire 'spectrum'? If one tells me it's a punishment, well, that I don't believe. God is an image of good and grace and purity and Him being evil contradicts all the teachings I came across. So don't tell me I have no place in this world because I'm gay or no place in your church if I like to fuck men. It is my right to find salvation and the beginning of that is to save me from myself and accept the way God intended me to be. I might end up in hell anyway, with all the prayers and punishments I subject myself to, but that is for me to deal with and does not concern your sorry ass. God is good and accepts us all, and if you think otherwise, maybe you venerate the wrong deity. It is me who has to come to terms with who I am and then make the step of sharing it with the world, but it's your close-mindedness, father, mother, and society, which stops me from being happy. But one day... oh! One day I'll find that strength and go on top of the world to smile upon you and thank you all for suppressing me for so long, for the courage and power your behavior had given me. I'm going to fly higher than any of my judges and bullies ever dreamt.

I vowed that night to work harder on my courage and devise a plan to strengthen it and my life foundation, be honest with me and others. But all in good time. I had to find myself that person, the half to share it all with and come out when the sense of security and belonging was not anchored in only one sea. I felt I needed more, and I ought to get it.

I updated my online dating profiles with pictures of my newly improved appearance – I was two sizes down and had a new haircut that showcased my thick brown hair – and approached the suitors with more confidence and more expectations. But, in the meantime, I wanted to keep myself at a safe distance from the pitfall of need and desire and choose carefully those I was to date. This attainment surfaced after a chat I had with a guy on one of the apps. I was talking about my insecurities and how my failed wannabe relationship affected me when he advised me to be honest with those I meet online, and with myself implicitly, if a serious relationship was what I was looking for. And so I started the quest.

I found myself being much more relaxed with my sexuality. It felt as I grew up. However, no life experience goes without leaving its mark on the participants. All the hate I encountered, the people I lost and found, the ones that stayed and supported me unknowingly, the jobs, the schools, my education, the commutes and travels, all came together and created the person I was. It was my time to shine and accept it all, good or bad.

After a week of scrutinizing profiles and men, I selected the one and accepted his proposal to go on a date. Tobias, a 4o years old German with piercing blue eyes and short, spiky blond hair, sugar-coated me and convinced me to go on a date. We set the meeting point in Soho Square, and he wanted to be the sole planner of the evening. So I just had to dress nice and be at the location at 6 pm on a Saturday.

I liked older men. Their age implies a sense of security, strength, maturity, balance, a wish of settling down and start a family, and experience when it came to sex and life – or I just fantasized it does. I often thought of my married neighbor, Matt, and how great a lover he would make if he was... well, different. I imagined a life with him once, and it just looked perfect, but the truth is I had to stop pretending I was living in a parallel universe and had to start living in the present. I had to get out of my head and meet real, tangible men.

As I like punctuality, I arrived at the meeting point thirty minutes earlier. I was, as always, nervous and sweaty. To my surprise, he showed up five minutes after me, dressed clean and casual in a white shirt with rolled-up sleeves, blue trousers, and lovely dark brown monk shoes. I like shoes, so those were the first I noticed right after checking out his prominent bulge, which dominated his groin area – I'm a bulge watcher, in case you were wondering.

I went in for a handshake to greet him, but he couldn't have it. Instead, he smiled and hugged me tenderly and voiced in almost a whisper how glad he is to have met me. He was taller than me and with a solid body, his muscly upper arms stressing the fabric of his body-fitted shirt. He reminded me of the Dublin Adonis. I felt inferior for a second, but his relaxed nature and calm, soothing voice made me loosen up. I wanted to make a good impression, so I tried my best to grow out of my shyness and be sociable.

Tobias had booked a table for us at a posh restaurant nearby, but first, he invited me for a first drink to get accustomed to each other and not have an awkward dinner. And so we went to a cocktail bar on Greek Street where he talked about himself and asked me all kinds of questions to get to know me better: about my origins, nationality, hobbies (which aren't many, to be honest), likes, and dislikes, food, my job.

Tobias worked as a cyber-security manager for a bank and lived in London for the past ten years. Nothing much but the ordinary type of man, a charming gentleman who never passed as gay in a million years – so manly and confident. He hypnotized me.

Two cocktails in, and an hour later, we made our way to the restaurant. He said, joking:

"You've passed the test, so now we can have dinner. Your innocence and obvious lack of experience with men make you the perfect candidate for more than a one-night stand."

His words made me smile, and for an evening, I forgot all about Liam and the other men about my town.

We had a nice dinner in an establishment I knew I couldn't fit. It was way too posh and quite expensive. Still, when I signed up for this date, I also prepared myself to pay my share of the bill even if I could not stop him from paying for the cocktails — being vegetarian and telling him about my diet prior to the date he had chosen a place that could accommodate both our needs. The menu was nicely structured for meat lovers and vegetarians alike. For starters, he ordered only three, instead of twelve, Maldon rock oysters, knowing I don't like any see related creatures, a couple of marmite mushroom éclairs, a small serving of tempura garden herbs with lemon yogurt, and a baked truffle cheese with crispy bread and onion jam. All watered down with Prosecco, which gets me drunk quite fast.

He had a whole baked Dover sole for his main, with butter sauce and chives, while I enjoyed a pea and mint barley risotto with radishes and feta. A bottle of chilled white wine accompanied the dishes to help us cool down in the heat of the evening. For dessert, we shared a chocolate and coffee mousse with an almond sponge and fresh raspberries.

All of this delicious food was accompanied by good conversation, and we hit it off quite well, in my opinion. I was glad that he was a smoker, so I didn't have to trouble myself with hiding it from him nor fight the urge to have a cigarette. After he paid the bill, we walked towards Piccadilly Circus to take the tube towards Putney. He lived in Fulham, and it was ideal for us to get closer to home and stop for a nightcap in a pub. We walked holding hands and stopped and kissed every ten feet. He was such a great kisser, but by his words, I was good too. The feeling of being wanted, appreciated and spoiled by this hunk, combined with one too many drinks, turned me on. I wanted him to have me then and there. I could feel his manhood poking and rubbing my navel every time he pulled me closer, holding me tight in his embrace, and kissed me passionately. I wanted that man to fuck my brains out of my head.

When we arrived at Parsons Green Station, we realized we had just missed the final order in the pub nearby, and he invited me to his place for a drink. I had conflicting thoughts about it: my urge for carnal satisfaction and the promise I made myself not to sleep with a man on the first date. I looked at him and took a moment to decide what to do when he, realizing my hesitation, said:

"Maybe this will help you make a decision…" and leaned in towards me, grabbing me by the face and kissed me deeply, pushing his tongue in my willing mouth. "So? What do you think? Wanna come to my place?"

"Yes. I'm convinced. Let's go," I said willingly.

He led the way from the station to his house. As a precaution, I needed to position myself and find known landmarks. We crossed Fulham Road, which I knew, and started walking on a side street towards the calmer residential area of the neighborhood. I was close to home and knew how to get there, which was soothing. I wanted to make sure I was at a safe distance from my house and knew my way there. I wasn't planning to spend the night with him. This meant concocting another lie for Suzanna and Thom to hide my second life, and I wouldn't say I liked lying to them. It did nothing but jeopardize our friendship.

We arrived in front of a house that looked the same as all the others on that street. The façades were painted white. I knew it would be hard finding this place again in the future. Tobias unlocked the door with one of his many keys and invited me in. Unfortunately, the hallway light was dim, so I couldn't analyze the interior as I wanted. All I could see was the basic layout of the entrance hall that led to a staircase on the left and a narrow passageway with two dark doorways on the right. After closing the door behind us, he pinned me to the wall and started kissing me eagerly. I gave in, letting my detective's eyes shut, and enjoyed the man in front of me. He grabbed me by my thighs, and in a swift move, lifted me in his arm, and after securing myself there by wrapping my legs around his waist, he carried me upstairs.

On our way up, between kisses and giggles, I noticed the framed pictures adorning the staircase. The framed black-and-white photographs depicted a family long gone, reminding me of the ones I saw in my grandmother's house as a kid. It felt out of place for a man like him to live in a house like that. The room we entered was almost empty, with just a wardrobe, a bed, a desk, and two side tables.

Lowering me on the floor, Tobias told me to make myself comfortable while he went and switched on the bedside lamps for a more romantic light. I took off my jeans jacket and removed my shoes, placing them under a chair in the door's proximity while my jacket rested on the backrest. He turned and faced me. He pulled me closer and started touching me, slowly increasing his grip with every short kiss he gave me. Trembling with desire and anticipation, I placed my palms on his rock-hard chest while he caressed my rear. I felt my pussy twitching with desire while wetting myself with pre-cum. Sometimes I just can't understand from where all this amount of pre-cum comes. I felt embarrassed, always getting naked in front of a man just to reveal a big fresh stain on my underwear.

He removed my top. I unbuttoned his white shirt to reveal a perfectly sculptured hairless torso. I kissed his neck and, moving down downwards his dick, I used my tongue to stimulate him. The savor of his skin joyed my taste buds. He was sweet and salty, firm and smooth.

Tobias sat on the edge of the bed and asked me to undress. I slowly lowered my pants and underwear in one move to avoid him seeing the stain, revealing myself to him in all my glory. He bit his lower lip while firmly squeezed his growing bulge. Then, standing up, he pressed me on the shoulders and guided me on my knees. With a firm grip of my hair, he pulled my head towards his still veiled junk and stuffed my face in his groin in slow motions. I felt his cock hard against my cheeks. I opened my mouth and tried to bite it through his pants playfully. It felt thick.

With both hands, I undid his belt and trousers, looking him in the eyes at all times. His grasp on my hair grew tighter, making my scalp hurt, but I went with it. I pulled down his garments to reveal the biggest and thickest cock I had ever seen. An image of the porn actor, Rocco, flashed before my eyes. I was afraid but willing to let him fuck me with that monster. I opened my mouth invitingly, sticking my tongue out just a fraction. No hands were needed; he positioned his pelvis so that his up-standing cock aligned with my mouth, and he pushed it in. Then, holding me by the back of my head, he gagged me with it. My jaw hurt as he commanded me to open it wider and put away my teeth. I felt his helmet-shaped knob opening my pharynx, blocking my airways. To stop myself from gagging, I held my breath for as much as I could just to allow him to fuck my mouth as he pleased.

I stopped myself from wanking, fearing a premature ejaculation that could spoil my drive. I loved the way he dominated me. He was in the known. He must have done it before, and I wasn't the one to tell him how to do it. Wanting him so much made me lower my guard and give myself to him as he wished.

He slapped my face and spat on it while fucking my mouth. I felt humiliated but enjoyed it.

Pulling me by the hair, he lifted me from the floor, pushed me on the bed, and told me to go on all fours. Next, he pressed my upper back down until my chest touched the mattress and told me to arch my back. Then, pulling my butt cheeks apart, he exposed my boy pussy and started spitting and licking and played with, making me moan and beg him to fuck me.

Covered in spit and lube, Tobias penetrated me with his massiveness, slowly. He might have been aware of his size and the damage he can do if not careful, so he took the time for me to open up and accept him all. I felt hot and cold shivers traveling fast throughout my body, from my sphincter to my penis, chest, face, and all the way to my scalp. My throat hurt from the abuse it took, turning my moans in barely audible gasps for air.

The speed of his thrusts increased, pushing me into agony and elation. I felt my muscles giving up, and I ended up lying on my front, powerless under his speed and strength. At the sight of my condition, he moved me further on the bed and climbed on top of me, between my legs, and penetrated me in one thrust. It hurt so much I screamed, but that did not stop him from resuming fucking me vigorously. I tried to turn and push him away as he grabbed my arm and, twisting it behind my back, I found myself pinned down, unable to stop him. Between the pain in my shoulder and the soreness in my ass, I felt euphoric. A solid need to ejaculate was building and building until I couldn't hold it in and squirted all over the sheets. The tension in my abdomen was so unbearable that I pushed Tobias out of me simultaneously. Seeing me shaking, he laughed and asked me with a sense of achievement:

"Did you just come? We are not done here yet. Do you want more, my beautiful boy?"

"Yes, Tobi…" I stopped to swallow and suppress the tickling in my throat. "I want more. But please let go of my arm. I won't push you away again, I promise." I said with a trembling voice while tears flooded my eyes.

I turned my face away from him, repositioned my ass, and biting the pillow, I waited for him to penetrate me again.

I ejaculated once more by the time he pulled himself off me. He looked pleased with himself and with my look; a glow in his eyes told me he enjoyed fucking me as much as I did him. He climbed on top of my chest and told me to open my mouth while stroking his cock. A jet of thick sperm exploded on my face. He growled and rushed to put his penis in my mouth and filled it with his juice. I swallowed. I was not too fond of the taste, but I did it anyway.

Exhausted, Tobias collapsed next to me and hugged me. He kissed me softly and whispered in my ear:

"You're the best I ever had. I hope you liked it too."

"I loved it!" I exclaimed.

As I sat there in his arms, I felt a euphoric heat inundating my body, and I said to myself: *I did love it.*

I needed to go to the toilet to pee and have a sip of water, but as I stood up from the bed, I felt my knees giving up, my legs' muscles twitched convulsively. I fell on the floor, on my knees. In less than a second, Tobias was next to me, pulling me up on the bed. He laughed and said:

"This is a sign of good sex. Don't be scared. You'll recover. I'll carry you to the toilet, and after you rest a bit, I'll get you a taxi. I want to make sure you arrive home in one piece."

"Thank you!" I said, smiling. "By the way, what time is it?"

"It just passed midnight."

"I should go now. My flatmates must be concerned."

"Don't they know you are in safe hands?" he asked quizzingly.

"Am I?" I said with a grin. "I can't even walk after escaping you."

He laughed at my joke and carried me in his arms to the bathroom at the end of the hallway.

He sat me down and told me if I needed help to call him back. After I peed, I stood up on my weakened feet and went to the sink to wash my face. Turning on the water, I noticed a rusty stain on the yellowish sink, created by a faulty faucet. Looking around me, I noticed there were not many personal belongings, like a toothbrush or perfume; just a new toothpaste, some untouched soaps, and a shampoo. I thought something was weird with this man but did not say anything. At the end of the day, I just met him, and he was nothing but excellent, as a person and in bed.

I walked with a bit of difficulty to the bedroom, passing by two bedrooms with their door closed. Tobias was waiting for me, already dressed. I personally wanted to have a shower to wash away the sticky fluids already dried on my body; they were pulling at my fur.

"Can I have your address so I can get you a cab?" he asked.

"I'll be fine. I will take an Uber. I have a discount code, so I might even get a free journey," I assured him with a smile.

"As you wish," he said, standing up.

Tobias approached me and hugged me lovingly, kissed me on the forehead, and asked:

"Will you go out with me again?"

"Of course. Yes," I voiced from his chest, where my head was buried. "What are you up to tomorrow?" I looked him in the eyes and winked.

"Hey, don't rush it," he laughed. "I'm going on a business trip to Germany for a couple of weeks but will be back. We can keep in touch and will arrange something."

I gave him my number and dressed. My driver arrived as I put my shoes on, so I rushed outside, forgetting to ask him for his number but thought he would text me fairly soon.

I arrived home just before 1 am. The house was quiet; Suzanna's bedroom door was shut close. I went and showered, scrubbed the dry patches of bodily fluids freeing my fur from the amber-like captivity. I threw the bathrobe on me and went into the kitchen upstairs. I ached for some honey tea to soothe my throat, and for a smoke.

Sat on the terrace, I checked my phone. I had many message notifications from dating apps, plus a few from Suzanna – she just wanted to check on me. After texting her that I arrived home safely (for her to read in the morning), I read the text from other men and decided not to reply to any of them. Tobias was still dominating my mind, body, senses. I was able to close my eyes and feel him inside me, taste his skin and cum, felt his touch, force, and firm body against mine. My ass was so sore it felt as I was still having sex. I said to myself: "What a man. What a body. What a cock!"

I wanted to text him but had no number, so I went back on the dating app we first matched on and realized he wasn't on my list anymore. Did he unmatch me already? What had happened? Was I just another one on his list, which he charmed and fucked on a first date and forgot all about after parting ways?

I shook my head to rid myself of the panicking thoughts that started piling up and went to bed. I knew he would text me soon… I hoped he would.

Thirteen

The following week, his text did not come. I wondered if I made the mistake of giving him the wrong number, but this worry turned into a more elaborate one: what was wrong with me that I could not keep or create a bond with a man?

My general mood was affected by my thoughts. I cried myself to sleep again every night, waking up swollen and tired every morning. At work, my performance decreased. I did not want to speak with anyone about my feelings, so I faked a smile whenever someone talked to me. At home, not being able to find a better explanation about my whereabouts on Saturday, I lied again and said that I met a girl at work and went out with her and that I was so under the weather due to her ghosting me.

I was fed up with how things went and all the worries, the lamentation, and low energy. Tobias dominated my thoughts day and night. I longed for him, his presence and touch, his adorable face and big manhood. I could not even bother myself looking on dating apps for someone new. I just swiped right with boredom and did not even reply to the messages I got from my matches.

I started living in my head again.

For a week, I did nothing but go to work tired and hangover just to make the money roll in so I can buy more wine and tobacco to fill in the emptiness left in my chest by my failures, and most of all by his silence.

That Friday, Thomas and Suzanna invited me to go for the weekend to Glastonbury to chill out and snap out of my misery. They insisted, but I was too tired and drunk to commit and decided it was better for me to stay home and feel like shit rather than be like that around them and spoil their weekend too.

On Saturday, I slept in. I woke up to an empty house around 11 am. My head was heavy, my eyes injected. I showered in an attempt to make myself feel better. As it happened to be home alone once more, I emptied my guts to be ready for an afternoon of dildo playing. The soreness of my buttrifice diminished considerably on Wednesday, and by Thursday evening, the residual feel of Tobias' skinflute was gone. I wanted it back so bad that I planned to recreate that night, on my bathroom floor, legs up and faux-cock in.

I went upstairs in my bathrobe, made a coffee, and opened a can of beer. I took my smokes and drinks outside. Looking at them on the table, I could not help but think of Carmen. She was the only person I knew to start her weekend with a coffee, a beer, and a smoke. I judged her for that at the time, and there I was, doing the same thing a year later.

I picked up my phone and went on dating apps. I was so needy and bored... I did not feel like hooking up but checked the market anyway. I found myself doing it out of habit, with no intention of meeting anyone when a guy messaged me. The conversation was short, a third line in, and I gave him my number. He called me. We agreed to meet in three hours at a pub in Fulham to have a drink. His Australian accent was strong, and I had to guess what he was saying, but in the end, I did a pretty good job deciphering his words, considering my headache was notable.

It was a hot summer day, so I put on some shorts, a t-shirt, and the only pair of runners I had; I did my hair and put on perfume – all involuntarily. I then went on the terrace and had another beer and a smoke when suddenly I realized I didn't even remember the face of the guy I was supposed to meet. What was I thinking? Why was I doing it anyway? I did not want another man… I wanted Tobias. Because I gave my word and said I'd meet him, so I went.

As planned, I arrived at the pub half an hour earlier than the meeting time and grabbed a beer. I wanted to mask the sour stench of my breath and the fact that I already drunk that day – smart move.

Oliver arrived ten minutes late, but I did not mind that. I was sipping my second pint by that time, and I felt drowsy. Luckily, I was inspired to go back on the app and check his photo, so I recognized him upon his arrival. But, unfortunately, he was not my type. Young, short, and boyish-looking, he did not spark any emotions inside me. I wondered once more why I was there, but no response surfaced.

He was a friendly and chatty guy, knew the game, and played it well. I tried covering my disinterest by asking him questions. However, I did not listen to his answers. I was so out of place that it exhausted me to keep focusing on some of the words he said in order to ask my next question. I have not realized how time flew. When he went to the toilet, I checked my phone and saw it was past seven. How did I manage to stay and look invested in the date for so many hours? When he came back, Oliver asked me:

"Fancy another pint?"

"No. Do you want to go to my place instead?" I found myself asking out of nowhere.

"That'll be nice. What would we be doing there?" Oliver smiled a devilish smile.

"Fuck. Maybe watch a movie. I don't know…" I said distantly.

"Yes, mate. Let's go."

Arriving home, I showed him into my bedroom and excused myself, and went to the bathroom. I brushed my teeth to rid myself of the burnt, embitter taste of smoke and beer. After washing my face, I studied it in the mirror for a while. I saw the emptiness in my eyes, dark circles accentuating my 'can't give a fuck' look and feel. I sat on the toilet and squirted to see if any shit was coming down the pipe. All clear - I was good to go. I then rinsed my crack over the bathtub, put my underwear and T-shirt back on, and went to the bedroom to find Oliver but-naked laying on my bed, with a smaller than average cock standing on attention.

"Surprise!" he said, smiling, and with a hand gesture invited me to sit next to him.

I went to my wardrobe, pulled out a box of condoms and some lube, sat on my belly at his feet, and started sucking him off. He moaned and grinned in delight while his eyes were closed, playing his fingers through my hair. Finally, he cummed in my mouth and pressed my head down on his pole until my lips cooped it all, touching its base. I did not bother swallowing. I was disappointed with his performance, but you know: shit happens. I crawled up in bed next to him and turned my back to allow him to hug me from behind. I couldn't look at him. I didn't want him there. He apologized for the premature ejaculation blaming it on lack of sex.

We sat in silence. I was thinking of Tobias while Oliver sweat-drenched my back and sheets. He was a large guy with small weak hands that sweated profusely, doing nothing. I was just fat and dry. The more I thought of Tobias, the hornier I became. My cock hardened, my ass cried for play. I started touching my sensitive nipples with one hand while with the other, I took hold of my penis and stroked it gently. Oliver took notice of my actions and laughed.

"I can't take a break, can I?" he asked.

I had no answer for him. All I wanted was silence. Tobias's image in my head was fragile, and any slight distraction could make it go away.

While touching myself, Oliver took the lube from the bedside table and, after squirting some in his hand, started fingering my butt and kissed my neck. Letting go of my cock, I arched my back and reached for his penis. He was hard again, so I handed him a condom and told him to fuck me. He went in in no time and started thrusting at a slow pace. It was better than his tiny fingers but not as good as a cock. I stood there with an empty look on my face – Tobias leaving me once again – and waited for the Aussie to cum. When he did, I told him to finger me more to help me cum as well. He obliged.

He was the second one to jump in the shower, so I told him I would wait upstairs on the terrace. I made us a coffee and sat with a smoke, I texted Suzanna to make sure they would not come home that evening. I sensed that Oliver wasn't about to leave any time soon, and I did not have the strength to kick him out. He joined me just to thank me for the sex, criticize my smoking habit, and preached about its devastating effects upon my heath. I zoned out during his monolog and lit another cigarette while he chin-wagged about cancers and bad smells.

When he finished, I invited him in to watch a movie. We went downstairs to my bedroom. I took my laptop, and after a short search on Prime, I played something I can't even remember. I didn't pay much attention to it, but Oliver seemed to enjoy himself. Halfway through the film, he paused it, took the laptop off my lap, and started kissing me. He wanted more sex, but I wasn't in the mood. Removing his clothes, he asked me to suck him again, and I did. He fingered my hole while I drooled on his balls.

Guiding me to stand on all fours, he went behind me like a horde-up bull and started fucking me relentlessly. I felt nothing but disgust as his sweat lingered down his body onto mine. He pushed and tried so hard that I gave up pushing back and let my corpse fell lazily frontwards. He climbed on me, continuing his fucking as I stood there under his weight, glued together by his sweat. I started suffocating. The air was hot and humid, and I felt as inhaling vapors coming off him. I faked enjoyment as much as I could, but I reached my limit. I pretended to be in pain and started screaming and begged him to stop.

"Does it hurt?" Oliver asked me, worried.

"Yes! Please stop," I said while tears poured down my face. They weren't tears of pain but disgust. I needed him off me, but I did not want to hurt his feelings. I apologized and offered to suck him off, to which he agreed. He came once more. We washed and went back to bed to finish the movie. I fell asleep at one point with Oliver next to me.

We woke up early the next day. It was a sunny Sunday, and upon opening my eyes, I saw a full round face with a big smile on it welcoming me back to reality. He kissed me and wished me a good morning. I stood up and went to brush my teeth. Upon returning to the bedroom, I offered him one of those single-use traveling toothbrushes I took from an event earlier in the year and sat back in bed. He came back washed and sat next to me. I felt like a prick when I realized what a good guy he was and what a cunt I was the night before.

To make things better and wash my sins, I went down on him and sucked him to completion as a morning gift. I did not enjoy it but did it anyway. Then, whit cum dripping off my chin, I told him:

"This was a thank you gift for last night," and I smiled.

"Let me return it. Lay on your back and…"

"No need," I interrupted him. "I wanted to do something nice for you. Do you fancy going out for breakfast? My treat."

"Oh, yes. That sounds awesome."

We went to one of the many coffee shops on Lower Richmond Road. I ordered avocado on toast with scrambled eggs and he, a full English breakfast. While we waited for the food to arrive, Oliver told me how much he enjoyed last night and how sorry he was for hurting me during the last fuck. I told him it was alright, that my vaginanus got sore from all the fingering and previous penetration.

As we sat and ate, he broke the silence once more and confessed that he was still living with his ex-boyfriend, but it was just provisory. He was soon to move to Islington with one of his friends. He was waiting for a room to become available in that flat. I choked on my sourdough when I realized he would soon live around my workplace. I needed to rid myself of him as quickly as possible. He could not be the one to break my protective bubble and spill my secret to the world. What would I do if I met him on the street when going out of work accompanied by Lala and Jakub? No way. I would not let that happen.

After breakfast, he asked me to go on a walk but told him I really needed to go home, sort out the flat, and get it ready for my flatmate's return. We parted ways, never to see each other again. He had no idea about it at the time and hoped to meet me again soon.

As I opened the flat's door my phone rang. As I extracted the phone out of my pocket, I thought: 'What a needy boy! Why is he calling me?'

To my surprise, it was an unknown number and not Oliver. I answered and heard the husky and calming voice of Tobias. My knees turned to jelly. My heart pumped faster. What a beautiful surprise!

Tobias apologized for calling me after a week of silence and told me how hectic his week had been. Meetings, business dinners, and symposiums exhausted him, but he had the time to call and chat with me as he had that Sunday off. I was delighted Tobias called, and I told him how much I missed him. He said he missed me too and couldn't wait to be back in London and see me.

As the conversation developed, he asked me what I would do to him when seeing him, how would I let down my barriers and let him fuck me and possess me. I started wanking my erected cock as he told me how he would tie my hands to the bedpost and lick me, head to toes, how I could not fight his massive cock bursting my cherry, making me cream over and over again.

When he hanged up the phone, my hands were covered in cum, my heart was full of joy, and I could not wait for the following weekend to come. I changed my bedsheets, did some laundry, and cooked dinner for Suzanna, Thom, and myself. I was in such a good mood that upon their return, Suzanna couldn't stop asking what I have done that weekend and what changed my disposition. Noticing the sheets drying on the terrace, she asked me cheekily if the girl from work came over for some sex. Shyly I admitted I had sex but made sure not to reveal that the girl was actually a man. I told her it went so well that weekend that I would spend next Saturday at her place. That day I proudly paved the road to a night of passion and sin with Tobias. She was so pleased for me that we decided to celebrate with a bottle of Prosecco.

Fourteen

The following week came and ended fast. Funny how time flies when you are happy. At work, I turned on my 80's music and danced and sang as cakes came out of the oven. Lala and Jakub loved my energy, laughed, and joined me in my craziness.

Every evening at home I cooked for myself and my flatmates. The food was high in fiber to ensure a clean colon for my upcoming date.

Tobias texted every night before going to sleep to tell me how much he was missing me and how impatient he was. Finally, we agreed to have a night in at his place. He would get all the supplies needed for a fun night while I insisted on bringing the wine.

On Friday, I took the time to shave my pubes and ass, made sure to put some moisturizer on to make my boy pussy smooth and inviting. I trimmed my beard and shaved my armpits, whitened my teeth, and went to bed early to facilitate the passing of time. Suzanna and Thom were to be home for the weekend, so I had to make sure to start my enema plenty of time in advance. I had no dinner on Friday to prevent any shit accidents – like the one in the hotel - on Saturday.

As the clock approached 8 pm, impatient and nervous, I started pacing up and down and around the house. Suzanna couldn't help herself and made fun of me. When Tobias sent me the meeting place, I rushed and grabbed the most expensive two bottles of wine I had ever bought, placed them in a tote bag, and ran out the door.

I met Tobias in Bishops Park. He was sat waiting on a bench. The evening air was warm, so I had my jacket in the bag next to the wine. I was dressed in shorts and a shirt while he was dressed more casually than the last time: a pair of dark jeans and a black V-neck T-shirt that was so tight on him it revealed his beautifully sculpted muscles. I could see his abs from a distance. I thanked the gods for him as I approached the bench.

At my sight, he jumped to his feet and extended his arms, and welcomed me with a warm and robust hug. We kissed as we were the only people left on the planet. His fresh smell and tobacco taste made my hair stand on end with anticipation. He took the bag off my shoulder. Taking my hand in his, we walked towards his place. After he told me about his weeks in Germany and me, about my weeks at work, I took the chance and asked him:

"Do you really live in that house?"

"What house? The one we are going now to?"

"Yes. And where we went last time. It seemed strange to see there were no personal belongings in your room or toothbrushes in the bathroom." My voice trembled.

"Well…" he laughed. "What a good detective you'll make." He paused for few seconds. Then, as we were approaching the house, he slowed down and continued: "Yes, I live there, but it's just for another month. It's a friend's house, and I stay with him until my house is ready. You see, three months ago, I bought my own place, and after I got the keys, I discovered there was mold everywhere. So I decided to refurbish the interior before moving in, and my friend was kind enough to allow me to stay in his late mother's house. I think you noticed the old, black and white photos on the walls… and the outdated furniture," he broke in laughter.

I laughed too and felt so stupid for speculating that he wasn't the person he showed me.

'I'm sorry I was suspicious,' I said with regret.

'Hey, don't even mention it,' Tobias said and stopped in front of the house, hugged me, and gave me a reassuring kiss. 'Let's go in and have some fun.'

He opened the door and invited me in, closing it shut behind us. The familiar hallway was better lit than last time, and I stopped to inspect the dusty frames on the wall. He laughed and started making fun of the old portraits. As we went upstairs, I heard some clatter and chatter coming from the kitchen downstairs.

"Don't worry. That's Ricky and his friend having supper. After that, they are to go clubbing, so we'll have the house to ourselves," Tobias assured me.

When I entered the bedroom, I was pleasantly surprised to see the effort he went through to make the night special: the bed had new black sheets on it, the room lit by candles placed on every flat surface in the room. On the bedside table, an array of lubes, poppers, and drinks awaited us.

He told me to undress, and so I did. I placed my clothes in a pile on the chair next to the door, my shoes underneath it. I was butt naked by the time he poured two glasses of wine. He handed me the drink and smiled, delighted at the sight of my nakedness.

"You're so fucking hot!" he exclaimed. "I have a present for you."

"What present?" I asked, intrigued.

"Hold this."

He gave me his glass and went to the built-in wardrobe door. With a stupid smile on my face that I could not wipe away, I watched him open the door on the other side of the room. To my surprise, there were no clothes on the hangers. Instead, the wardrobe housed just a black suitcase with a small red ribbon tight to the handle. He took it out and closed the door. Unzipping the front pocket of the suitcase, he watched me smiling. He slowly pulled out a shiny black gift bag with some black tissue paper sticking out of it. He took his glass from my hand and gave me the bag. I kissed him shortly and thanked him, and sat down on the edge of the bed. With shaky hands, I removed the tissue paper and peeked inside to see some fabric. I looked at him inquiringly; he replied with a smile. As I pulled the fabric out, I realized it was a pink pair of jockstraps.

"I want you to wear them tonight."

"Thank you, my beautiful man!" I said, jumping in his arms and kissed him.

"I don't want your cock to come between us today. So tonight, you'll be my whore, and I'm going to fuck you as you deserve. When I finish with you, you'll never want other men but me," he said in a severe tone.

"Yes, daddy." I said, giggling.

"Put those on while I go downstairs to bring some ice for our drinks. It's going to be a hot evening, and we'll need it."

"OK."

"And by the bed, you'll find a lube pump and some poppers. Squirt some lube deep in your vagina and sniff some poppers. You'll need them if you want to survive the evening."

As he left the room, I put on my new jockstrap. I took the pump that looked like an anal douche but thinner and smaller and placed the narrow nozzle deep in my rectum. Squeezing the rubber end, it released a good amount of lube inside me, feeling the cool thick solution invading my cavity.

I decided to say no to poppers. They made me drowsy, and I did not like them. Also, I didn't enjoy them when Liam pushed them in my nose.

I threw myself in the middle of the bed on all fours. Placing my knees wide apart, I curved my back, pushed my ass up, and lowered my chest and face on the fresh-smelling bed sheets. As I heard footsteps approaching, with the corner of my eyes I notice a shiny silver chain hanging from the corner of the headboard. I had no time to investigate. I wanted Tobias to find me ready for fun.

As he entered the room, he exclaimed:

"Good boy! Stay there now. I'm coming for you."

He placed the bowl of ice on the desk, downed his glass of wine, and removed his clothes. I peeked from my frog position to watch him. I shivered at the sight of him naked. What a gorgeous hung man!

Tobias came behind me and slapped my butt with both palms using all his force and weight. I cried a high pitch cry. It hurt. I could feel my skin burning as he placed his hands on my buns and spread them open to reveal my rosette. He spat on it and started licking it. The feel of his tongue on my goodie hole made my cock stiff, and a cascade of pre-cum stained my pink jockstrap. I didn't care. I clenched the sheets and enjoyed the pleasure. His strong, long fingers followed shortly. He firstly put in just one to make my whole worm up and loosen. When the second finger joined the party, I felt euphoric and thought of how higher the pleasure could get when his massive cock would stretch my hole.

"I can see you used the lube. Good boy! Do you want daddy's cock inside you, boy?" he asked me in his husky voice.

"Yes, daddy..." I moaned.

"Come, suck daddy first," Tobias commanded.

He came in front of me and sat on the pillows, spreading his legs on either side of me. I laid on the bed and wrapped my hand around his prick. I slowly licked its head.

Pushing up the foreskin, I stuck my tongue underneath it. With circular motions, I liked the head all-around, increasing the speed as I went. The resounding noise he made and the twitch of his body shown me he loved it. When he couldn't take it anymore, Tobias pushed my head down, forcing his penis inside my mouth.

"No hands!" he shouted. "Open up your mouth and take it all!"

I did as I was told. Tobias was more dominant and commanding than all the men I had in my life. I assumed that my passiveness and submissive behavior came from my lack of experience in the bedroom. I felt the knob extending my throat, and I gagged. I fought to push back and gasp for air, but he was stronger. He forced himself inside my mouth until my chin touched his balls. At that moment, I was glad I had no food that day; otherwise, I would have puked all over him. He eased the pressure on my head and allowed me to breathe. I looked at him, slobber drooling down my chin, and saw him smile. I sucked him more, but this time he let me do it my way as I forced myself to swallow it all without his help.

When he had enough, he grabbed me by the hair and pulled me off him. He stood up on the bed and pulled me to my knees in an upright position. His fully erected phallus pirouetted in front of my eyes. With swift movements of his torso, he then slapped me on the mouth with it while commanding me to stick out my tongue. A firm slap on the face followed, which made my eyes water. He was more aggressive than the last time.

"Do you want to get fucked by daddy?"

"Yes…" I whispered.

"Louder!" he shouted.

"Yes, daddy!" I said.

"Are you mine tonight? Can daddy do whatever he pleases with you?"

"Yes, daddy."

"Are you my slut, faggot?"

"I'm all yours, Tobias."

"Good. I'm gonna rape that ass like no one fucked it before," he said, delighted.

As I stood there on my knees, him pulling my head backward by the hair to look at him, his cock on my face, I started fingering my ass to warm my sphincter up so I could welcome him inside me without resistance.

Grabbing me by the neck, he pushed me on my back and climbed on top of me. I put my legs around him as he kissed me, still holding a tight grip on my neck. He guided his dick to my pussy with the other hand, and in a thrust, he penetrated it. I screamed in pain as I felt a muscle rip. He didn't stop. He fucked me slow and deep.

Arching my back, I caught a glimpse of the door with the corner of my eye. It was open.

"The door…" I moaned with pleasure and pain. "The door is open."

"Shut up!" he roared while pushing his wood deeper.

"They can hear us," I said worryingly.

He placed a hand on my mouth and nose, stopping me from breathing, and said:

"Let them hear you scream, whore! Let them watch us."

Let them watch us? I thought. Were his friends still home? Were they listening or, even worst, watching us?

Tobias stopped smacking my whole and, resting inside me, he asked if I would allow him to tie me to the bed. I thought of the chains I saw earlier and remembered our first conversation when he described how he wanted to fuck me.

Looking at him, in his blue and sparkly eyes, I nodded approval. I could not resist his charm. He was so beautiful.

He stood up from the bed and went towards the headboard, and told me to lay on my front, position the two pillows under my navel, and stretch my arms upwards, which I did.

"I've never done this before," I confessed. "Do we need a safe word, a password, or something?" I asked with a grin.

He smiled and said:

"Don't worry about it. Just let yourself go, and I'll take care of you. It may hurt at times, but I promise you, you'll enjoy it."

At the sound of his reassuring voice, I gave him my right wrist. At the ends of the silver chain was a wide strip of black strong-looking fabric, with artificial fur padding, terminating in a long Velcro sheet. He tied up my right arm and went on the other side of the bed to secure the left one. The chain was in one piece, fasten to the bed through metal rods with a loop at the end, and it was long enough that I was able to touch my face with one arm at a time, giving me some sort of freedom.

As he moved towards the end of the bed, I asked him to close the door, but he ignored me. My heart started beating faster as the panic and regret settled in. What was I thinking? Why did I allow this man to take complete control of my body? I felt uncomfortable and restless.

The panic hit harder when Tobias took hold of my ankles and secured them in the same manner as my hands. I was completely immobilized, and the adrenaline rushed through my body, awakening my senses. I asked him for a sip of water as my mouth was dry. Instead, he lifted me and gave me few sips of wine with ice in it.

"Wait here," he said and went out of the room. I thought it was a stupid thing to say to someone bound to the bed and laughed a nervous laugh.

After a short time, Tobias came back in the room carrying a portable Bluetooth speaker, playing electronic music. He opened the black suitcase, produced a sleep eye mask like those you get on an airplane, and covered my eyes. He then turned up the speaker's volume, pushed an open bottle of poppers to my nose, and told me to sniff.

With a head-rush, I waited for him to come behind me and fuck me again. As I laid there, a smell of cigarette smoke reached my nose. He offered me to take some puffs, which helped to calm me down. Then, I heard him pacing around the room. He poured another glass of wine and smoked. The sound of a belt buckle made me twitch, and I knew what was to come and hoped he would have a sense of mercy when hitting me with it.

The leather belt slapped me with a bang. I felt my fat ass exploding with pain. A cold and then hot shiver surged throughout my body. I screamed. He didn't stop. He slapped me repetitively as I twisted and turned, trying to hide my bottom from him, but I couldn't go anywhere under the circumstances. I shouted and begged him to stop, but he didn't. He continued slapping me with the belt for a further minute or so.

When he stopped, he threw the belt on the floor and took a fresh ice cube from the bowl he recently replenished and soothed the hot, sensitive skin on my fesses. I felt the tightness in my muscles disappearing under the cool treatment. He placed the melting ice cube on my hole and told me to relax and open it up, but I refused. I did not want a piece of ice in my rectum. Disobeying him was a bad idea. He forced three fingers inside my crack and, opening my butt hole pushed the cube inside. It was followed by three more. The paralyzing coldness turned into cramps, and I fought him as much as I could so I could squirt the ice out of me. Finally, Tobias stopped the torture and helped me squirt the ice out.

"Now you are tight like a virgin," he laughed.

He sat at the top of the bed, catching my arms underneath his legs, and told me to suck him. His cock was flaccid and sticky from the residual body fluids accumulated doing the first fuck. I realized he did not cum the first time, so I planned on doing my best to make him finish so I could get my freedom back. I blindly searched with my tongue for the tip of his pole and liked it. I took him inside my mouth and used my cheeks and throat to stimulate him and get him hard again. I resurrected him in no time and continued forcing him deep in my mouth while he moaned and stroked my head. My skin was sensitive from the poppers, and even my scalp produced a wave of electricity that accumulated in my cock and sphincters, making me crave more of him.

My arms went numb under the weight of his legs, but I continued sucking him and did not complain. As I was doing him, I pushed myself up on my knees and arched my back to signal him how much I wanted him to fuck me again. Suddenly, I felt a pair of hands pulling my ass apart and a tongue rimming me. I tried to jump from underneath Tobias's legs with the intent of removing the mask of my eyes and look at the person behind me but couldn't move. I was pinned down. I freed my mouth and shouted to them to stop and set me free, but all I did was worsen my situation.

"Shut the fuck up!" Tobias shouted at me while pulling hard at my hair. "You gave yourself to me completely, remember? My friends here are bored and horny and want a piece of you, so you better give them what they want, or you'll regret it. Do you understand?"

"No. Please!" I said through clenched teeth and started crying. "Please don't! I don't want this…I beg you, let me go!" I cried out.

"Shut up and suck my cock, you fucking slut!" he said as he pushed his cock inside my mouth and fucked it deep, depriving me of air.

The second man penetrated me and started thrusting deep and forceful, my sore ass hurting me more. As my oxygen came in tranches between gagging and spitting, I couldn't protest more. All I did was choke on tears and dick while being fucked in the ass by a stranger.

When they stopped, I heard them talking:

"Joe, it's your turn," Ricky said in a broad German accent.

"Yes, man! Look at that pussy, so fucking juicy!" Joe said and spat on my crack. He sounded Irish.

"Go fuck his mouth. He's an expert." Tobias told Ricky.

As they coordinated themselves around the room, I managed to take off the mask and looked at them. As I tried to release my hand from the bond by pulling hard, I caught a glimpse of the two strangers. Ricky was shorter than the others, covered in greyish hair, with a short goatee, a prominent belly, and overall muscular and thick. His metal cock ring caught my eye as I couldn't help but look at his penis: it was average in size but thick. Joe was tall and ginger, with the characteristic crystal white skin covered in ink. His cock was comparatively bigger than the others. I cringed at the thought of him fucking me. That would hurt and definitely destroy my insides.

I started screaming for help, but they shut me up fast. Then, finally, a punch in the liver made me gasp for air, and I curled up as much as I could. As Joe pushed himself inside me, I howled in pain once more, but my opened mouth did nothing but allowed Ricky's cock easy access.

I couldn't stop myself from crying. I felt tortured and humiliated by those men. I feared for my life when Tobias threatened to kill me if I don't shut up and do what I was told. I wondered if that was to be the end of me. A simple gay Romanian gypsy wanting to love and be loved, met his maker in a dusty old house under the power and abuse of three men.

I continued to fight them whenever a surge in energy and adrenaline allowed it, but I grew tired, and my muscles gave up on me. I forced and pulled at the hand bondages until my wrists hurt and felt as dislocating them.

Ultimately I gave up. I let them do whatever they pleased, and at the sight of me not resisting them anymore, Tobias asked me:

'Will you behave if I set you free?'

I nodded in agreement. He unfastened the Velcro cuffs, and they all stopped. I laid there in bed, stroking my wrists just to realize they were failing me. I had no power to move them much. My ankles were covered in threads of blood, sore from the friction I subjected them to while pulling at the cuffs. I gently put one hand behind my back to touch my aching hole, wiped some of the froth, and looked at it. It was pink with blood.

The three men laughed at my behavior. Joe took a cigarette from the pack, lit it, and gave it to me. I sat in the middle of the bed and inhaled deep. I felt a step closer to freedom. Tobias stroked my cheek lovingly and handed me a glass of wine. It was red and cheap. I recognized the bottle. I smoked in silence and wiped the tears off my face. When I finished, I stubbed out the cigarette in the ashtray given to me by Joe and asked in a trembling, low voice:

"Can I please go home?"

"The night is young, my love. And we are not done with you," Tobias grinned. "And don't forget: the more you struggle, the harder it will be for you. So do what you're told, and maybe I'll let you live."

A knot settled in my throat at the sound of his words. I was about to die. Fuck.

Fifteen

I was exhausted. After the short break in which I smoked and drank some wine, the three men stroked their cock and brought them back to life. With tears and saliva drooling down my chin, I sucked them all, jumping from one phallus to another. The more I sucked, the drier my mouth went.

My soul was numbed. My mind stopped processing what was happening to me. They took their turn to fuck me in different positions and with extra vigor. As the night went on, the pleasure vanished in thin air. The only thing that made me go on was my wish to satisfy them and save myself from certain death.

I wanted to die before and came very close to hanging myself, but something stopped me then. Maybe the same something made me push on that night. I didn't want to die without feeling the true love of a man, but how on earth could I find that when at the moment I offered myself to one, I got raped. I did not want to die without seeing my parents, dog, and friends once more. I had to stay focused and find a way out of that house. I tried remembering if I disclosed my address to Tobias, which I haven't, so home was the safe place I had to run to. I told myself to stay strong and avoid pissing them off. *Comply and stay strong, you stupid cunt!* I kept repeating to myself on and on as they pulled and fucked me like savages.

I could not comprehend their virility. It felt like hours went by, and they did not cum once. Or have I missed it?

The moment came, and the first to jizz inside my ass was Tobias, followed by Ricky. After that, the devilish Joe had to fuck me some more. He even lit a cigarette while doing it, laughing madly at the cheers of his friends. He finally cummed, deep and plentiful. I felt my prostate giving up under the pressure of his massive pole. As he stood there, his prick inside my pussy, Tobias wanked me hard. A fast stream of cum exploded from my penis onto the sheets. It felt like I have peed a kidney stone, but something felt good for the first time in a long night. From standing on all fours, I collapsed on the bed, sore and tired. They laughed triumphantly, and Joe stubbed his cigarette on one of my butt cheeks. I screamed, but he grabbed me by the neck and strangled me to silence.

Seeing my face changing color, Tobias forced Joe off me. I fought for air and coughed my lungs out.

I curled up in the fetus position, my knees touching my chin, closed my eyes, and cried.

"Hey, fucker! What are you doing?" Tobias shouted at one of them. "Don't pee on the bed!"

I suddenly felt the hot urine stream washing my shoulder and back.

"It's rented, Jürgen! No one will be here tomorrow," Ricky said in his broad German accent.

Jürgen?! What did that mean, I asked myself as the men offered me a golden shower. All the cuts and rashes I had on my body stung at the contact with the salty urine, but I did not twitch.

Shortly, Ricky and Joe left the room, leaving me just with Tobias. He squatted down near the bed and, stroking my urine-soaked hair, said in a calm voice:

"I hope you enjoyed it as much as we did. It appears you weren't ready for us. I should have given you a safe word. Too late now, right?"

I burst into tears. He smiled.

"Don't go anywhere. I'll shower and then will take you to the bathroom to wash. You're a mess."

He left me alone in the room. I was alone. It took me a moment to compose myself and gather my strength. The remorse and pain turned into anger. I was angry with myself for allowing someone to take such advantage of me, for trusting a fucking stranger, for my obsession with finding true love in the arms of a man I knew nothing about. What a stupid, irrational cunt! What a waste of air I was!

Maybe I should have stayed there and wait for them to finish what they started, to kill me. But I was too angry with myself to wait. I took my clothes from the chair in one hand and searched for my phone in a rush. I founded it in the pocket of my trousers. Good news: the clock was twenty to four.

"The devil's hour is over," I said to myself and creped down the hallway and onto the stairs. I heard the shower running in the bathroom upstairs and realized that Tobias was still washing. As I reached the bottom of the staircase, I looked over the railing towards the kitchen. Ricky and Joe, butt naked, ate at the kitchen island, chatting and having a good time. I looked towards the entrance door to see if the key was in the lock. It was not. Fuck.

Hoping for the best and praying for a bit of luck, I took my chance, crawled to the door, and tried it. It opened.

That was the first time I ran in years. I never ran for the bus, but this was no bus. This was my life, and I had to run for it. So, dressed in just the pink jockstrap, with no shoes – Fuck, I left my boots behind! – I ran. A few feet away from the door, I stumbled and fell, scratching my palms and knees. It did not matter. I stood up and rushed as fast as I possibly could to put some distance between myself and the house of horrors.

Entering the park, I went and hid behind a big tree. While putting my clothes on, I kept an eye on the road as a precaution. I looked for my keys in the pockets, took them out, and arranged them between my fingers in the eventuality of meeting someone on the road and had to defend myself, and sprinted towards the bridge.

To this day, I have no idea from where I had the strength to do it, but after what seemed 5000 miles of running, I arrived in front of my building. As I stopped to catch my breath and calm myself – thinking the danger was over and no one followed me – I noticed the stench coming from my hair: a sour smell of sweat and ammonia.

I unlocked the front door and walked inside. I had to move slowly and quietly to avoid waking up my neighbors and my flatmates.

In the end, I made it to my room where, after removing all of my clothes, I stuffed them in a plastic bag and pushed them underneath the bed. I had a look at my face in the mirror and noticed minor bruises on my neck and chest. The punch in the liver left its mark too. The bruise was as big as an opened palm and violet in color. I turned around and looked at my ass in awe: it was dark brown with dashes of purple and red, raw skin popping out in patches. The cigarette bur hurt the most. My ankles were bleeding, as was my heart.

***

As I crossed the mountains, on my way from the airport, I looked at the sky. It was closer than ever. The clouds played around the snowy peaks inviting me to join them. But I couldn't be bothered.

In the past week, my bruises turned a darker color and shrunk. My wounds had scarred, but my heart was crushed and my spirit torn apart by the recent events. I was healing but only on the outside.

I was grateful for my boss's understanding and him approving such a short notice holiday. I lied to him and everyone else that my grandfather died and I had to go home for his funeral. They believed me.

When Suzanna and Thom saw me that Sunday, they were shocked and asked me many questions about the bruises on my neck – I was able to conceal the others – but I assured them they were nothing but love bites. I blamed the wine and lack of sleep for my shot eyes and darkened face. I lied about the date that it went great until the morning when she broke my heart by telling me how much she disliked me, how awful I was as a lover, justifying my low energy and degrading mood. They believed me.

For a week, I contemplated my existence, my worth, my life, and my adventures. But, unfortunately, nothing was worth living for. So I took this holiday and called it "my purgatory."

Arriving home, I hugged and kissed my mother and father, played with the dog, and lied some more about my fabulous new life in England, when in fact, it was shit. All I wanted from London was the freedom to be who I was, the freedom to love whom I wanted, the freedom to express myself and to live an honest life. I was a liar.

I blamed myself for not achieving any of that. I loved London, but that wasn't enough anymore. I did not love my life nor myself. The men I met did nothing but fed me illusions of love and happiness and took small parts of me with them every time we kissed or fucked, leaving behind an empty carcass covered in spit and urine that no one else wanted. I regretted fleeing my rapists' house that night. I should have stayed and let those three men finish what they started. I was weak and worthless.

The flight home was a procession in which I made peace with myself and signed my death sentence. As my parents went to bed that night, I creped in the attic, the place of my teenage years. I removed the two loose floorboards in the far right corner to unveil my damnation. It was a dusty and weathered shoebox from which I took out a sealed letter addressed to my mum and a rope. The time has come for me to put an end to this madness. I was weak.

Bursting into tears, I clenched the letter and rope to my chest and thought of my parents finding me hanging from a beam, and could not help myself but feel their pain. Would it be selfish of me to give up not thinking of the chaos I might leave behind?

Then, Carmen's words surfaced from my mind's abyss: *a man like you will die alone.* Could I let her be right?

For the first time in months, I turned my face to God and asked him one more time: 'What was I to do with the life You gave me. What?'

Don't miss the second book of this series which tracks the rise of Thomas in Romania and London.

The men about my city

Coming 2022 in hardback, paperback and ebook. Subscribe to the newsletter at **www.thomasolorr.co.uk** or follow the Instagram page @thomolorr for updates.

If you enjoyed this book, don't hesitate to leave a review on Amazon. Thank you.

Printed in Great Britain
by Amazon